Empire of Dreams

Also by Giannina Braschi:

Yo-Yo Boing!
United States of Banana

Empire of Dreams

Giannina Braschi

A new translation by Tess O'Dwyer

Printed in the United States of America.

Empire of Dreams by Giannina Braschi was first published in 1988 by Editorial Anthropos in Barcelona, Spain, as *El imperio de los sueños*. It was first published in English by Yale University Press in 1994. New translation by Tess O'Dwyer first published in English in 2011 by AmazonCrossing.

Translated from the Spanish by Tess O'Dwyer.

Published by AmazonCrossing
P.O. Box 400818
Las Vegas, NV 89140

ISBN-13: 9781611090659
ISBN-10: 1611090652
Library of Congress Control Number: 2011904663

Empire of Dreams

Translator's Note

The only way to know precisely what an author means is to become the author. The translator becomes the author the way an actor becomes the character. Memorizing the lines in Spanish and reciting the words as if they were my own, I traded in my voice for the dramatic voices of the lyric "I" whose adventures and emotional states vary from book to book in *Empire of Dreams.* Swapping names, ages, nationalities, and genders, Giannina Braschi's characters are a cast of actors playing the roles of other characters. As a translator, I tried out for every part.

In *Book of Clowns and Buffoons,* I played the fortune-teller who predicted the past, the magician who torched his audience, the drunkard who cried in a room full of bottles, and the little lead soldier who marched against the smoke of the city. In *Pastoral; or, The Inquisition of Memories,* I was Shepherd Giannina, who led a revolution in New York City. It was chaos. Cows and sheep were grazing the sidewalks as shepherds took over St. Patrick's Cathedral and the Empire State Building. I nearly lost my voice screaming through a loudspeaker, "Now we do whatever we please. Whatever we please. Whatever we damn well please!" The roles grew more complex as I made my way through *The Intimate Diary of Solitude.* There I played the writer Giannina Braschi, who played the writer Mariquita Samper, who played the writer Berta Singerman and an array of other characters. With red-dyed hair, surgically implanted freckles, and a gold tooth, I especially enjoyed the role of the fairy drag queen. But the most gratifying moment was when I shot the Narrator of the Latin American Boom, who kept rewriting my diary. He was such a nuisance. Always telling me what to think, what to do, what to write! Once he was out of the way, my thoughts flowed freely onto the pages. By the end of *Empire of Dreams*, I had lived so many lives that I no longer felt I was a character. I was all of them and, therefore, the author herself. I fancied myself annoyed that Giannina Braschi had translated *Empire of Dreams* into Spanish before I had the opportunity to write it in English. I thought of all my transformations. Were they in vain? I became the actor who became the character who became the author. Now what was I to become? The translator. And how was I to do it? With the respect that great literature deserves: faithfully.

Translating as close to the literal edge as the flow of the prose allowed, whenever possible I used word-for-word replacements, which rolled into rhythms of their own, inciting brilliant images and luscious sounds. More often than not, however, the poems demanded thought-to-thought correspondences, as the Spanish is proverbial and idiomatic. Because each poem builds on another, as does each book, word choice depended on a context larger than individual poems (especially when translating recurring images and phrases). As for the transliteration of Giannina's non-words, it was simply a matter of ear. For instance, the wheel of fortune in *Song of Nothingness* was "chis-chassing" when it should have been "click-clacking." Likewise, horns were "cras-crassing" when they should have been "bee-bopping," while dogs were "buff-buffing," and they should have been "wuff-wuffing." Witnessing my symbiotic relationship to her text, Giannina invited me to edit the Spanish manuscripts, which she believed she had "overcorrected." We collaborated. She reviewed drafts of the translation to encourage "musicality and intensity," and I reviewed drafts of the originals to rid the poems of self-censuring. Together we reinstated lines and poems and rearranged the sequence of the Spanish edition. We widened the circumference of inclusion in this translation. It contains poems that have not been published elsewhere. For the most part, our collaboration was harmonious; that is not to say that there was no contention over interpretation. Sometimes an egg is an egg is an egg. Other times, an egg is a ball is a day. I could not always distinguish one egg from another. She, of course, always could. At a poetry reading years ago, we read a selection from *Poems of the World* which included a mutual favorite beginning with the line "Eggs are months and days too…" I had always enjoyed its affirmation of plurality, its false logic, and its musicality. The eggs were so clearly a female symbol of creation that the slang connotation of *huevos* (testicles/balls) did not occur to me. When Giannina read her "Huevos," the audience broke into laughter and applause in the middle of the reading. A woman next to me shook her head in disapproval, muttering, "*!Qué sucio!*" (Smut!) If I were not so curious, I would have skipped the poem to save myself some embarrassment. Instead, I read with all the confidence I could feign. Afterwards, the woman who had muttered, "*!Qué sucio!*" thanked me, saying, "Yours was sweeter." Failure confirmed. Humiliated, I blamed Giannina: "Why did you let me lay eggs when they were supposed to be balls? You should have told me *huevos* means 'balls.'" Annoyed, she replied, "Do you mean that your 'eggs' doesn't mean my 'balls'?" Then, in the heat of the moment, she taught me a few more slang expressions. *Poner un huevo* literally means "to lay an egg." Figuratively it means "to make a mistake." Rendering an idiom literally is just as fatal an egg as taking one too many liberties. I believe I have acted responsibly with my translator's and poetic licenses, which have allowed me to save what must always be saved across language boundaries, sometimes at the expense of abandoning slang and puns: the spirit of the poetry, its rhythm and run. Not only does a translation have to sound like the original, it must be an original. That I learned from José Vázquez-Amaral, who introduced me to this work.

I met Amaral in the autumn of 1985 when he was professor emeritus at Rutgers University and I was an undergraduate student. He was from the Spanish Department, and I was from the English Department. Aside from the New Brunswick campus, our common ground was a love for modernism. Amaral had introduced Ezra Pound to the Spanish-speaking world with his translations, *Cantares completos (I-CXX)* and *El arte de la poesía*. I visited the retired man of letters expecting to spend the afternoon hearing stories about Pound and Joyce. What I heard was this: "I've struck another world treasure." Amaral said this as he handed me several spiral notebooks and a stack of pages torn from yellow legal pads. "After twenty-two years of [translating] *The Cantos*, I thought I had fulfilled my aspirations. Then I read this." He pointed to those yellow pages. The handwriting was like none I had ever seen. "So angular, so determined. Hieroglyphics," I thought. "Pound and Eliot brought us the twentieth century. This poet carries us into the twenty-first century," Amaral told me. "Who is he?" I asked. He smiled. "Giannina. Giannina Braschi." Amaral had drafted an English version of *Empire of Dreams* and asked me to join him in revising it. He was confident that some poems "took off and soared in draft one," while the rest were grounded, "flapping, frustrated." There were plenty of obstacles to overcome. As the original was a work in progress, nearly half of his drafts did not correspond to the final manuscript. Most of what did correspond were inspiring sketches of his ideas to come. In 1986, when his health was failing, he bestowed upon me Giannina's yellow pages and his spiral notebooks. "Take over," he told me. "Let Giannina scream, and kick, and punch, and cry. Let her laugh. She is always laughing. And know that she thinks. She is always thinking."

I. Assault on Time

And take upon's the mystery of things,
As if we were God's spies.

—Shakespeare, *King Lear,* act 5, scene 3

Behind the word is silence. Behind what sounds is the door. There is a back and a fold hiding in everything. And what was approaching fell and stopped far away in proximity. An expression falls asleep and rises. And what was over there returns. It's a way to put the world back in its place. And something comes back when it should remain remembering.

But if I ring the bell, water jumps and a river falls out of the water again. And the body rises and shakes. And the rock wakes and says I sing. And a hand turns into a kerchief. And twilight and wind are companions. And this twilight appears amid lightning. Outside there is a bird and a branch and a tree and that lightning. Above all, there is noon without form. And suddenly everything acquires movement. Two travelers meet and their shoes dance. And breeze and morning clash. And the seagull runs and the rabbit flies. And runs and runs, and the current ran. Behind what runs is life. Behind that silence is the door.

Hello. Since you came back late I forgot that I'd written you a line, but I remembered that the line from the book had picked up a paper you sent me so that I'd jot down a memory for the book. You've forgotten the commas again. No, I haven't. They forgot to end memory with a period. I remembered memory when I could no longer write to her. But then I was afraid to insist. She hasn't come back yet. If she doesn't come back, I'll have to erase page five. Memory was on the guest list. But I forgot her telephone number. Then I walked to eighth avenue of page three and suddenly met forgetfulness. I crossed the avenue on page ten and saw the horizon of page three and erased the night. Now I'm on the day of page five. Forgetfulness dropped by unannounced. I wasn't expecting to find you on the way. I thought you would stop by on page thirty. But you're early. I'm sitting to the left of this book. We talk.

A letter comes and visits me. Puts its legs up in the living room. Wanders about speechless. Suddenly it explodes and another shape appears. Welcome! It flees swiftly, and I see two, three, four, five, seven, five hundred letters. Suddenly I hear the word *river* and water runs in another river's space. I repeat *river* two, three, four, five, seven, five hundred times, and cold imprisons twilight. Then this letter's twin slope trembles. There is no return without reaching bottom. The letter is born of life. That's where its limit began. I discover the world underneath.

Letters are not letters because they dream. Something barely traces them, like a hand. These letters are not signs of another sign. The letter's rhythmic beat, when counting syllables, is life spelling its memories. And we stop at letters, hiding in the darkness of their syllables. And we say, I've lived five years in this letter. Here I forged a first syllable and a last silence. I forged enigmas and secrets too. From my letter, the way was born. And from my letter, the beginning and the current of other letters attached their syllables to the name. And I tell myself: each letter is an old memory and a silence.

No lagoon is darker or clearer or fuller of mountains or planes than the first letter of your name. I said that I was made entirely of letters, and I used to say that the horizon would turn clouds into other signs, revealing other letters. But I didn't say that behind all those letters the horizon cuts the edge of my hand.

Everything I'm searching for is underwater. There are no flat surfaces there. I'm not searching for the oblique or what glows at night. By day I escape all insinuation, all effect and consequence. I love water, but I run away when it brings an ambiguous current. I know something about what flows, what comes, and what sometimes touches. That's when water, turned into rock, sings. And when it reaches the mouth of the river, it knows that point is called calm. No stories or tales are told there.

I must admit that everything I see today is cloudy and round as a crystal ball. Now I feel the current advancing from never and changing into the always of your port. Port hoping to become more of a port when it plunges into my water. As if it had no other outlet than to sail through the water. And, of course, everything is a welcoming farewell.

Sit down. Think and look at me. Not at me, I'm not the one who wants to see you sitting down. Look at the truth. I don't want to see the sea. Calm down. Give me your hand. That's the way the sea calms down. Sleep. Now feel how the waves calm down. And tomorrow the landscape will change. Rock, water, sea. What's the use of sitting down? Quit hinting that the gaze will close again. Rid your body of the past. Breathe. You're sailing again, and you're only thirty. Understand me. It's not youth. I'm leaving. You want to go. But we stay.

Behind the word is silence, and behind that silence is forgetfulness. I didn't understand the silence or that letter which thought that line, because I couldn't remember the forgotten. And there, far away, the horizon. I fell silent. Silence fell and the work spoke. They spoke. I stretched out my hand. "Why didn't you tell me I had to begin anew? Behind what sounds is the door." And I grew sober. I raised my hand and pointed to another silence and another line. "Behind the word is silence." I lowered my hand. And then there were doors, silences, forgetfulness, letters, lines.

I'm speaking. Speak to me. I hear you. I'm in a hurry. I need for us to make love. In a looser way. Open your arms. If you see me correct a verb, write me an accent and make me shut up. I don't want to interrupt your quiet time. But give me a call or drop me a line. I have to ask accents their permission. Someone took my accent, wrote a comma, and left. Left me alone. Tell your word I can't inhabit it today. It will have to be tomorrow. Listen. You have to obey the meaning of the phrase. "And what does it mean to speak?" I said to you. And I grew sober again. And you said, "Now you laugh," without telling me you had to close your eyes when you slept. And you said, "Now sleep." And when you called me again, I closed the door halfway. "Open up," you said. And I shut it with a period.

The day jumped today. I'm upside down, it said to me, and I answered, help me take the ceiling down and put it in the street. Then bring the ladder over here and lay it on the floor. If this is how the world is, I said to myself, so be it. But then the phone rang, the alarm rang, the clocks all rang, and everything escaped. Even my shirt wanted to breathe. Open me, it said, and I obeyed. It's already been two days of surprises. Yesterday I wanted to break away and I escaped. My hand was placed elsewhere. Your rebellion, you explained, is that you pick up the pieces. Yes, everything should stay in its place.

But we have to go, we have to run. We should go back to what you warned me about. But what goes around comes around. It came round and flew. It came back in asleep and then sat down. What was asleep was shaped like a hand. Suddenly it ran to the opposite corner and escaped. Are there hands? I asked. There must have been hands if we were caught up in hellos and goodbyes. Goodbye. Pleased to meet you. But the hand came back. And everything escaped.

The day is not okay. It's like saying that I touch the table and find it in the same place where I couldn't find it on the day that was okay. And today is a nice day for a walk, but I'll stay here. And it's okay for the windows to be open so the wind comes in. And for the table to come out with me for a stroll because it wanted to learn to walk. I doubt it'll find its way back because when we left the street wasn't in the same place, and I think the day was annoyed with me because I told it that nothing had changed.

The day told me that the wind had returned to my house. And had to leave because a man who wanted to build a new day came looking for it. But when the wind came back to see me, it dressed up as a new day so no one would come back to find it. And the wind took off again when the phone rang. The wind didn't know how to tell the day that things were no longer in their place. And the day told me that when the wind returned to my house the ladder no longer had rungs. And I was waiting for someone to tell me why there were no stairs. But the wind disguised itself as a doorman and told me he didn't know the house was mine. So, I told the day, things are no longer in their place. And the day told me the house was mine, like the world.

The wind and I would have to take off and fly. Behind the closets and under the furniture no one says my name. Yes, I know I'm in a world of invisible sounds. I know its origin. I go toward it and hide. The wind and I would have to take off and fly. My hand says it no longer feels the air.

And among countless roads and old shoes, among countless objects and questions, the hand acts as an interpreter and the air keeps blowing and the door keeps unlocking and the wind goes back to its place as the door closes. Yes, everything has its place and everything counts when objects empty at the door. But I feel there is something weightless that runs. It's something that rises and never reveals itself and has to hide in some other corner. And that something now raises the same questions. And the wind finds itself back at a point—right where silences fly and objects jump back into the painting. By then you can't tell one object from another—it's as if they weren't the same objects: watch, mirror, image, wind. But my hand knows the fall, and there's no other question than the same objects striking the frame and the chair. And the air stays still and everything is in its place.

Sure, it's true. Questions don't change the truth. But they give it motion. They focus my truth from another angle. And you said: we're cleaning up the truth. We must clarify certain things.

You don't tell the truth and your jacket eventually comes back made of another material, and your shoes say sure! and run back to you telling my truth. Even if it's raining now, your truth may be that it's not raining inside like it's raining outside. Though silent you may be saying what I'm thinking when you weren't talking. Don't pay attention to me and keep saying *come* when you said *go*. Then don't expect me to listen when you say *come*. You'll come with your words *get out* and the door will open. I hear those words and the door opens halfway. Then you'll come and I'll know how to say: *get out*.

I always knew that a bit farther or closer but never in the exact spot a heart beats at the bottom of a painting and we are the breaking glass. I don't reach as far inside as I told you and I see you reflected in a sliding mirror and you open your eyes forgetting that you look at me and I am forgetfulness. But there was a time when to the left of the heart and at the end of the road to the heart and in the river and the street of the heart and within the walls of the heart you slipped and railed and spilled and always came back different through the heart, moving the heart and plunging into that heart. And you went so deep inside me that I asked you to take me in the dark and in the light—and inside that heart and your pulse and your nerve. Now there is no need to break the heart's glass because it was submerged, full.

You tell me to say things as they are and I say them as they were and you say I changed them and I say I'm not changing them because that's the way they are. It all depends on how they get up. But it's not that—things get up when I make them. I insist, I'm not planning anything. They get up without a clock, and like sound they fall. And that's the way they are because that's the way they were born. They are happy when I get angry. They sit down when you get up. They fall asleep when I'm awake. But don't wake them when I'm up or call them when I'm asleep. And understand me. It's not a command. Understand them, not me who commands you. It's the mandate of things. I'm not forcing you to obey them. They are in charge. And the table's place takes the chair's place, and the chair has a body's place. And goodbye because you get everywhere with distance. Not because my goodbye, which doesn't obey you either, is against goodbyes. And yes, because I took my goodbye from you and I'm hoping you'll hold it against your own goodbye. Goodbye and goodbye.

I arrive at your house transformed into art, framed behind my memories. The lintel's color is the guardian of my dream, you the painting. The frame of your house crosses the bottom of the painting. I cross the horizon and sit down to look at it. I arrive home transformed into art, framed behind your memories.

I learn more in those seven days than I already know. And if that day draws near, I wish to know Mondays and Thursdays. When that Thursday fades away, I ask for Saturday. The slowness of that Saturday makes me wish for Monday. And this Monday I find that Friday begins by thinking about you, and this Friday I learn that I draw away from you again on Monday, and every Monday with you brings the same hours as Tuesdays, Wednesdays, and Saturdays. And I'll never return to that Sunday that drew me so near to your distance.

There's no such thing as more or less. Hours are in excess. I'm constantly walking and counting as I go: one, two. Three hours have passed. If I multiply them, days run too. Then I make a circle and break it. The sea breaks, and those four and these two broke. You couldn't, we couldn't. The hand will close that circle when you come. What hand? Don't look at me. I'd like to tear the number from the waves. Look at me. I have five fingers, and the waves are five. What does this five know of that seven or ten! Don't you know if I open my fingers I count fifty and say, five, five? My fingers can't open, they close. They run through the waves and always return to the sea. And they come, they come back without knowing their secret. They take what they bring. They bring the sea and take the embrace. Count the fingers on my hands. Ten fingers add up to twenty embraces. And day falls and so does that embrace. Don't open love if the embrace is closed. Open the wind and close your hand. Keep away from my kingdom. The wind wanted to say the opposite. But the air took off with that hand.

What's the use of memory, says the alarm. You have to love. You have to love when the heart is alarmed. And that alarm is the keeper of fire. And water can't quench the fire loved with alarm. So who cares if the firemen arrive. Water turns into more flames. And then the bell rings. You won't come, I said to myself, you didn't show up with the bell. And suddenly that alarm is on fire. And you come in, slowly, and not even the bell knows the surprise.

Ask. I don't ask for much. I only ask you for two numbers, two people, two accounts, two ways, two mirrors, two words, two gazes, two digits that always add up to four on a mirror, that always add up to eight and answer us, count. There's only two of us, you and I together. Ask. I don't ask for much. But for what little I ask the mirror repeats only two are left: you and me.

It's impossible to be everywhere. You always said that. The impossible is possible in our framework. But you break the frame of another impossible: me. And I break the frame of another pronoun: you. And even if that frame be made of you and me—an impossible, a lip, some gates, a bar. Within the possible there is no impossible that won't pierce the me and the you: the frame. And you and I have reached the bottom.

I was wrong, it's true, I made a mistake. But it's great to be wrong. Excuse me, lady, I don't mean to bother you, but I like to watch you walk. Excuse me, sir, I didn't mean to interrupt, but I'd like to say: goodnight. Now I can breathe. And I'd like you to tell me why I can't walk if I'm here, or why I couldn't talk if I were over there. But I like being called when I'm absent and always answer: here I am. And we like to remember the road I did not tread. That means: I like to walk when I stay right here. And when we go for a walk I'll say to myself, the day is different when it stays home. But I don't like the one who keeps saying: come back when you say I back off. I didn't love the one who told me: back off, but then you told me to come closer.

I know a night that always came close, and it came so close that it opened my doors. On entering I saw that it carried memories in the deepest part. Quiet on the threshold, the noise of another distant night sounded. That one could slip in because it was hot and the door was open. Even the wind snuck through the legs of that nearby night.

For a while that night and I were walking along deserted streets with no stores. Night grew weary because it knew that I never reached the end of the street. Sometimes it would look at me as if it remembered the way of another distant night. Once more the wind snuck through my legs. We got lost in the city of the wind. But another nearby night was opening in the middle of a crowd.

For now, a pair of dark glasses warns me that night has no windshield. Happiness is solitary. I know an elephant is listening to me and a raven is repeating my words from an oblique angle. Meanwhile, I divest myself of all my whims. The elephant is afraid. The raven said so when we returned from another dream.

Then a hat said that it can't resist the wind because it's awake. A window opened its pane at the end of the day, and a drop of dew insisted that spring was on its way. But spring replays the same song. Not a cherry stirs behind it. Nostalgia is a fruit with the pain of distance in its pit.

There's something so dark about night. I shut my eyes tight and dream in clarity when I look at it. Night is not that dark. It's not the blackness. It's something as obscure as fire. And it lifts me. When they open their eyes, night and fire know one another. But they're not the same. And now I get up and look at you. There's no darkness and no fire. And silence must be dark. And day will bring different fires.

Hold the arrow's circle, you used to say to me, like a hand that only has five fingers. I got it, I answered. The arrow crossing the horizon is drinking the dream of the gods. Don't confuse the terms, you used to say to me. The hand that only has five fingers robbed me of the enigma.

I already told you I'm not rushing, I'm waiting. I know I'm not rushing because I'm not thinking about night when I'm walking. I'm walking as if the day were eternal. That's how it is. If it weren't so there would be less roads. But you can't tell what is less when you're waiting for a night that never comes. There you have it, you say, just what you were expecting. No, that's not it, I say. I say what I was thinking when I was walking. Now I can't go back. Getting there is not the same as having waited. It's not the same as night, but it has the same slow pace as exhaustion. The door loses its support. It lost the way of hope just like me. I told you I can't return when the road has four letters: STOP.

From two slow roads, two fast stops, I take the wind. The body belongs to me, I take the day. I'll never stop, the road will stop, we'll take a quick look from two slow roads. When I plunge into thought, I walk at the foot of the wind. If I have penetrated something, it's only to be alone with all I see. To avoid looking at it, I think of another foot. I don't want to see day, or night, or that hat. To avoid resting, I run. Like the plane that flies and the car that stops now. A door closes and night rises. Streets are crowding solitude.

Nonetheless, solitude doesn't span our hands or move like waves. Each wave brings a different rhythm, each morning is new. The breeze doesn't move like a window, doesn't think body, and doesn't feel alone. But my solitude would like to say day and says far away and says now and thinks tomorrow inside. It knows there will no dialogue tomorrow because there will be no memory and its windows will be shut. But if I said fire, there would be no other truth than water and a forest would continue correcting the words. My water wouldn't know how to repeat what fire said. My hand, then, would span a dialogue, yours throws back the question, and the monologue hides its word. And, nonetheless, my silence raises the question and the man doesn't answer. A sign questions me and the word opens. There is no shore.

I'd have to wear a different heart, a new joy, a new outcome. Mystery could be assaulted without breaking its tide, I mean, without feeling anything. The stone would petrify, and even sad shyness would become daring, if it knew that a memory was watching it. Ignore this eye and that door. I don't want you to feel it or see me. The movement of the tide is different when you look at it. The eye of the window loses its transparency if the wind shuts it. Solitude has no enigma when it stays alone. But when your heart is a party, solitude becomes crowded with memories. Ignore this eye and that door. I don't want you to feel it or see me.

When I look at the road I always find the window, and then I stop looking at it so that it will join me. And I forget. Then I suspect that nothing is there. Later I discover the floor. And they stick together. Later on they meet the eye of the sea. To join horizons, it's enough to recognize them. Face to face without the interference of distance. So you won't know what you saw and remember something else. The road must always divide its ups and downs. They are always two—someone has told me that water closes the circle of three. For me at least, it's always two. Afterward, the world disappears.

I was coming back through the outcome when I found the entrance. I didn't want to go back to the same street, so I went another way. Maybe I felt the curve is shorter when it doesn't tell the entrance that it will come with the outcome. I don't know, I asked the street for the unlisted address. It didn't feel abandoned. I knew it when it folded its hand. But soon it put its finger on the return and insisted that the very first was the long way that mentioned the beginning without realizing it. What's the use of being in the fifth dimension? I told the first of all not to mention it to the last. I promised to keep distant. I would have remembered the promise of that address. I would have sent it another way. I would have made it promise me another beginning. The prompt answer was slowing down. What's the use of knowing the first or ignoring the next-to-last, if the next-to-last didn't remember that the outcome would take place later? If it were any less sincere, I don't know. It doesn't matter and it's not going to matter, the others told me. You still don't know the way? I can only send you to another one. But I don't know, I really don't know. Ask the sidewalks, that's what they're for, let them go with you. The car would probably fight it. But, at least, the sidewalk put up a fence and divided the paths.

Now that the paths diverge, I'd like to measure the distance. It's not the distance of the foot when it meets the hand, nor the silence of the head or the death of the heart. How many friends are there? How many can count on the measure of silence? If they encounter death in the middle of the night, they greet her. That's all. And enough. Repeat it. They greet her. I count them among the others, brothers. Don't leave me here. I don't want to meet the dividing line because I divided the paths and the hand went with the leg. Where is it? they asked. Where did it go? It hasn't left. It's sitting with the foot. And now the leg is nonexistent. The noise of the hand is non-existent. How do you think it can walk without the hand? Here is reality. The hand touches distance. Touches it, nothing more. That's all. And enough.

II. Profane Comedy

Dedication and Warning

This book is dedicated to the entire cast of Profane Comedy. *To the actors who play the roles of drunkards and buffoons. It is also dedicated to all the people I do not mention but who helped me with the setting of the stage and the costumes of the actors. I must thank all of you for having listened to my poems. This book was written to be sung and to be read in public and to be heard by large audiences. And to be proclaimed at festivals and gala concerts. With elegant dresses. And makeup. And actors. And extras. And comedies. It was written for carnivals and orgies. It was written for well-being and joy. And it was written for the company. It was written for the world and for life and for crowds and masses. It was written for elitists and thinkers and philosophers. It is the book of exclamations and interjections. And it is the book of Bacchus and Faustus. And of the poet-child. And of the poet-actor. And of the poet-philosopher. All these poets and the poems never written by philosophers are in the pages of this book. And children's stories are here. And the prima donna is here. And the singer. And here is Giannina, dressed like a clown, giving the right cues to all the actors of* Profane Comedy. *They are all nervous and will soon begin to sing their complaints and their laments. Soon the alarm will sound. Soon* Profane Comedy *will begin. Soon fortune-tellers and buffoons will speak. Soon* Pastoral *will arrive. And soon* Profane Comedy *will end.*

1. Book of Clowns and Buffoons

...et la Reine, la Sorcière qui allume sa braise
dans le pot de terre, ne voudra jamais nous
raconter ce que'elle sait, et que nous ignorons.

—Rimbaud, *Illuminations*

You'll open the door to poetry because poetry doesn't know what it's looking for and asks for the shade of light and asks for the river and the sea and eats cherries off the tree. Poetry spy and watchman of trees and mountains, and thief of the secret and of the mysteries pent in glass, and drunkenness of night mourning for the widowhood of day. Poetry of the telegram and poetry of the telephone. Poetry of the letter in the mailbox. Poetry of the envelope and the melon eaten by love's wound. Poetry between the peach and the airplane's letter. Poetry between you and me. Poetry between he already came and left and disappeared, between the fruit and the seed bearing the message from the lover who won't come back.

Poetry of a shark with two whales and a scarecrow. Poetry of a crab and a turtle. Poetry of an elevator and two cars. Poetry of a giant and a dwarf. Poetry of the clown and the drunkard. Poetry of the star and the wall. Poetry of the summer and the mountain. Poetry of the flying rabbit and the dancing shoe. And poetry of the pain of joy and poetry of the joy of pain. Poetry of the bat and the witch. Poetry of the torn shoe and the barefoot stockings and the horizon that looks for you when you're approaching the mountain. And poetry of the hill you descend when you're expecting the call. And poetry of the number lost in the magician's hat. And poetry of the parakeet's feather and poetry of the parrot and the parasol. And poetry of the shadow and the witness. And poetry of the accident and the surprise. And poetry of the love that never arrives because it escapes with the magician's hat. And the word *poetry*, and the sound *poetry*, and the shadow *poetry* become two real numbers, two real clowns, two jumbo jets, two cheers that no one hears because shattered in the air they cease being air and shattered against the wind they cease being wind. And poetry without mountain and without hill. And poetry without absence and without emptiness. And poetry of the night and the witness in shadow, in dust, in nothing.

Poetry is this screaming madwoman. Everything seems poetry. Madmen gaze high. Everything seems madness. Madmen fear no moon, fear no fire. Burns of flesh are poetry. Madmen's wounds are poetry. The witch's crime was poetry. Magic knew how to find its poetry. The star wasn't poetry before the madwoman discovered it. Discovery of fire in the star. Discovery of water with sand. Neither poetry nor prose. Salt is for fish, salt is for death, the poem is not among the dead. Remember, but don't write it. Love her duendes and act as her Lazarus, but don't wake her. Sleepwalker among cats, thief among dogs, man among women, woman among men, blasphemous toward religion, fed up with poverty. Tear out poetry's voice. Don't let her find you, hide. Disregard her, ignore her, forsake her. Don't touch her wounds, she'll scorn you. Back away. Scorn the poem. Develop without her. Give her the necessary distance. Let her feel conceited. Then insult her for not having written with power. Deride her dreams, slap her eyes. Kneel down and ask her forgiveness. Take the poem from her belly. Sleep beside her, but don't avert your eyes. Listen to what she tells you in dreams. Acknowledge her when you see her spell the names of hell. Descend with her into hell, climb her streets, burn within her history. There are no names, no history. The volcano erupts and rushes toward the poem. I can't do anything but bash her against a rock. I can't do anything but embrace her. I can't do anything but insult her dreams, and she can't do anything but open the poem for me, just a crack, a crack in silence, without watch-men or maidens, with a fowl and an owl to keep distant, to keep silent, to show up barefoot. And she couldn't do anything but crash against the rocks, and the wind couldn't do anything but blow her locks, and time couldn't do anything but eternalize her moment. And poetry is nowhere in the castle. She disappears through the trapdoor, escapes with the fire that burns her and dissolves in water.

I have been a fortune-teller. Ages ago, I told the fortune of buffoons and madmen. You remember. I had a small voice like a grain of sand and enormous hands. Madmen walked over my hands. I told them the truth. I could never lie to them. And now I am sorry. Ages ago, a drunkard filled with dreams asked me to dance. I used my cards to tell his fortune when his drinks became blows. My banging on the door killed the sea. Memories finished us. Madmen and buffoons count the grains of sand and have never destroyed night's dreams. They draw up the night and rise filled with middays. Magicians were and always will be my companions. Without guessing their tricks I started fire in their throats. But none explode. Maybe one. And with the fish another chimera rises.

The circus had a white elephant and a red turtle. All my enemies are drunkards and friends of my body. Only they open the doors of my eyes and suck, suck ten kilos of love and gulp, gulp fourteen kilos of chimeras. Stars forewarn me of ten years and predict twenty more. And the owl sits on my smaller arm. And the madman intimidates it. And drunkards ask for shade. Too many cards about too many chimeras. Take the bottle and raise it. Let us toast in the name of tricks. Then the magician emerged from another side of me, lifted his shadow, and destroyed the drunkard. Hot and cold conversations create words in color from all angles of my body. Shadow arches frame this scene. Drunkards will fill their bottles with other stories that buffoons are planning around the border of this painting. There's only a black chimera left drinking the liquor of stars. And a fortune-teller sitting on the stairs.

It was true and it was a lie, too. That's why I got drunk, said the buffoon sitting on the stairs. The fortune-teller suddenly arose and told the buffoon, the stars divined it, it was written in the cards. King of spades and buffoon do not mix, added the madman leaning against the door. Everyone except me, said the madman, is looking at the future of the sea. But the sea is a king without a sword. That's why he is sitting on the stairs next to the buffoon. Here are the cards, said the fortune-teller. Here is the king without a sword, with his wicked card. Here died the drunkard with his bottle. Here is the screaming madman, with his wells full of water, searching an empty orbit.

I am the magician. Back away! Here is the trick. You see it from a distance because you can't see it up close. Come closer. You look for it in my hands and the trick escapes between my legs. Don't look at my legs. The trick isn't on the stairs. The trick is that flying bird. The spectators stood up hoping to see the flight and see the magician on the stairs. Suddenly ten firemen arrive with their big slickers and hoses. Back away! Back away! Come closer! Come closer! The trick was that flying bird, and the spectators stood up and asked: What's going on? No one answered them. Then they saw that the bird had already left. And they asked again: What returns? Then there was a fire and the magician vanished. When the lights blacked out, then, and only then, the bird with a fallen wing came forward to the edge of the stage and cried out: Victory! Victory! I have burned the spectators.

We'll play another theatrical scene. It consists of one act, divided into three parts. We: leading actor. You: stage director. I'm the audience. Open curtain: four chairs and a ladder lost in the dark. The ladder, the ladder, says the director. The chair, the chair, breaks in the leading actor. The curtain falls. The lights go out. The curtain rises again. One can be in the front of this theater listening and laughing: I am, we are, all laughing. And the curtain falls on this play. And the desert, I'm thirsty, I forgot the words. Please don't tear silence from me. Let me escape quietly. The lights have stopped looking at me. I feel like setting myself on fire. Firemen of the night, get me out of here. Cut, cut, said the director. Let's wind it up.

Adventurous and silent actor, filling himself with mouths and faces, with an absent-minded look, open hands, double-dealing anger, lies and shams in just one secret, intrigue of a handkerchief, with fewer dreams, checking his hat for the trick with the scarecrow and the mirror. And parting with everything that cuts, cutting his orange in halves, lifting his head, doubling his fracas, looking for his return and hiding from the world, emerging and exposing his whole body, cut between hand and foot, cut between night and morning, with a closed fist and a grain of mustard, filling himself with stars, cutting corners, with his hands on night, and his mouth in sorrow, in the station of the port, in the house of the world, in the tree of the hand, in the fist of the sand.

I want to be rid of this corpse that murders my soul. I have other things to say. Get away from me. Leave me alone. I request another name, another clown. Too many buffoons, too many dead dwarves. I want a giant. Get out of my body. Don't take the corpse from me, let it walk away. Swing with the trapeze, glide. Make me a shoe or nail the sole into me. Become a sock and wear me. I have a nickel for the dance and the comedy. You see, that's just what I was telling you. I have no comedies. Kill me if you want. But do for me the black, the white, the void. Absence, as though it were the death of absence. As though absence could drop dead, dead. Of course, the corpse is a stick that walks. Of course, the stick gives you a blow on the head. Of course, you should never play with death.

With both lined up four abreast, she read me the cards. Poor drunkard of the tale. Two fortune-tellers dead. And a room full of bottles. The clown is drunk. And the cards of death wait on him. His snout is blue, and he looks like a bear. And the rag doll of death—you can't love him like this—with the clown flinging him by the arm—madness. Because he is drunk and has no river or breakdown. Because they cork him in, unable to love him. Because stars no longer love him.

I'm sitting on this page, between one line and another, between a buffoon and another clown, between two syllables, and I jump up, and touch the page with the tip of my finger, and throw it into the basket. And I look at it, and become a basket, and repent. And I start to cough, and throw the ball, and pick it up. And I kiss the sky, lifting my arm to fall to the floor, torn, and to rise and cry out. And I'm restless. I need to throw the ball away, so I can lose the page, and then I can laugh or cry. Whatever happens, nothing matters. Because I sleep, dream, awaken, weep, kiss your left cheek, and walk slow, walk fast, where are you, I call you and hide and find you and knock you to the ground, we undress and backtrack, it's the safest way, the star is waking, and the moon is crying to the earth that constantly watches her. Because the sun won't come out, there is no noon, and the orange is locked in its rind, and the snail tucks into its shell, and the world stays inside its house. And we look at one another, sad, mad, and we don't know what to say. Later Mom will come to wake us. Brother, quiet, quiet. The earth yawns because it isn't sleepy.

Giving me your hand, you pick it up to frame it. Darting into the street, you're run over by an oncoming car. Throwing myself into the basket, I turn into an ashtray and touch the cigarette. Collapsing into the tomb, I sleep, sleep. Opening the closets, I say enough, enough. Closing them, I'm left sad, sad in a closet. Opening the sadness of the closet, I lift four and I'm left with two. Even and uneven, brother, they'll always be brothers. Widowers from the orphanage, the uneven, squared. The sled is triangular. The uneven say so. Heavens and stars repeat it. The worm and the snail and the tree shout it. The uneven is crying. Stars console him. Nights wake him. The piano destroys him: duende and mermaid, gnome and deer. Four, uneven: paired. I dive into the slide. And I grow and awaken. Five years, ten even, twelve tied. Three brothers.

I touch everything, to add it up, and subtract ten, four more. Five loners and ten kings, two swords. The fortune-teller and her wicked deck. Heavens and stars play solitaire. I know it, I'll know how to say it. I'll flip the cards, check them, and close my hands. Two swords cross the hand of the fortune-teller. And cards don't lie. Widower, I will be, you will be, four stars and two cats fighting in every street, a worm. And a crystal ball, rolling luck, hitting the ball, ten blows, two falls. At night, in the streets of death, between the sun and the fortune-teller, ten cards, two lies. I understand, a blackened eye is worthless, and the stars pass and return regardless.

In all corners and squares and circles, just one heart, prophecy of five hearts and a loner on the road, and a drunkard without a bottle, sober from madness, solemn and hidden. Widower of two stars and a road. Three corners opening the drunkard's eyes, stars and chimeras, and rivers of sadness. No one is laughing. The drunkard keeps him company, and the bottle heals his wounds. There is a square corner on the road of two. Looking for you in four, company, I am two. Corner of the third, I am another, less ten. I understand your fall, but I am five, not ten. Understand the hill, they are twenty, never two. I understand, a blackened eye is worthless, and the same stars pass and return regardless.

A mob of witches and killers. You look like an idiot, the hat doesn't have ears, the street doesn't have legs, buildings don't walk, obscurities don't talk. Idiot, you have a tongue, speak. You idiot, I was on the verge of speaking. I fell deaf—said the killer. Birds don't sit, dogs don't kneel, bats don't shrug. Idiot, shoulders are shrugged. You idiot, I hope the witches destroy the fire. Killers have blocked my aqueducts. I speak for the killers, cops never ask anything. I raise the possibility of the question. You idiot, not even wolves howl. Ask Little Red Riding Hood, it was a flood of machine guns and rifles, she told me so. I thought they'd kill me. You idiot, not the killers, the cops. And I turned my back on them.

Treason, treason, treason. Death, death, death. Ecstatic bewitching throat, fire is blind, blind, blind. Vanish chimney. Smoke-filled eyes. Fire. Crime-covered hands. Duel of the godfather and the pirate. The sword, the dungeon. I see a beacon of black butterflies. The crime has vampire eyes. Cassandra conducts the orchestra. Joan, the mad witch, groans. Someone round has committed a crime. Someone perpendicular to the base of the triangle has emptied the stream. The prodigious crime has destroyed the stores. Omen! Omen! the witch cried out. Ecstasy, ecstasy, the comic tragedy. The earth quakes, the news, the omen, the prodigious crime. Dwarves of the prodigy, rabbits of the syringe nurse, ambulance of the dancing trapeze artist, fire of turtles, flash of pain, fencing duel, caveman, fireman, gas mask, bomb, pliers of the crab.

Hysteria, I have a dead son in the belly of the city. My mourning is the edge of the world. I have both navels empty in the center. My mother abandoned me. I'm raising the belly of the city. I gather pigs, the breeding ground of mourning. There is no belly, pedestrian, there is no belly, transitory wind. I scream at the top of my lungs, my lever is the parachute of life. I hear you, fertile belly. I examine your limbs, electric organism, ventriloquist. Marionette woman, sleight of hand creature, the wolf married grief, and Little Red Riding Hood's grandmother fled crying out to the murderers. You bitch, cold hysteria. Neither the policeman nor his motorcycle stop you. But I stop you. Halt, cold hysteria! Halt!

Laughter, laughter, laughter, I'm happy, I dance, because you're crazy, unsettled, I'm lost in a world. You said world, I understand, I see world. Hell. I don't feel you. I've stopped thinking. I felt cold. And I went wild, dancing in a cardboard tumbler. I wiped it out, erased the line, animal, only you remain. It was twelve. I'll be back in five minutes. No, please, let me sleep. Ocean, I need to find out. Returning eye, go away. I am asleep. Approaching eye. Back off. Please, I need to sleep. Anesthesia, I keep lizard hours, but please, I don't have a centaur's tail. I'm not a dragon or a giraffe. I'm finished. I need some sleep. Lifeless, no, I'm not that old, but tell, tell the lizard, I love. And even if the tail is fire. Prove it with kisses. C'mon, I dare you. Coward. I try to erase the line twice. The giraffe's line or laughter's? No, the centaur's line with a dragon's tail. I mean, the giraffe. Unsettled. The dead man rises. Poor thing! Let him sleep. I am asleep. Not me, not me. Please, corpse, leave me alone, I beg you: let me sleep.

I vanished, I almost became wind, phantoms are not white. Recognize them, I told you. Learn to vanish. Don't fly so high. Keep sleeping on the stairs next to the drunkard. What are you talking about? Don't you understand me anymore? What are you asking me? It's been two days, speak to me. I'm listening. And we're not two elevators, let's face it, we don't have buttons or buildings anymore, we don't even have seas or deserts. The streets have spoken to me four times. The fifth time, I'll shut them up. Traffic, the red light says walk, the green, stop. Traffic is submissive, solitary. Policemen are firemen, ambulances are the ambivalence of danger! Danger! Hysteria told you to halt! And halt! arrested me. Life is coffee made from rainwater. The house's hat is not a chimney. Steam, evaporate. I subtract three months from March to December. The addition of two zeros, see you later, see you later. The door up in flames, and the garbage asking for the corpse. The world chatting with the dialogue. And life at the railroad station emitting smoke, unsettled, the months of the world's train and the gates of the northern hemisphere.

Happiness is the quiet hand, don't you see it flying, happiness is crazy, I see it near the couch, sitting, rising, flying, leaf falling to the ground, and floating up again, I see it floating near the river, fishing for turtles. Happiness. The killer's hand, the Sunday turtledove, as Papa had a canary and Miguelito had a parrot. And I loved Bracho. And I played turtles with Juan. Edmée! Edmée! Juan hit me with the racquet. Bracho, we're near the tennis court. They look at us, we hit the balls, they send them back, the racquet got angry at me. Can you believe it, the world, no, not the world. Pilo, come with me, follow me. Mama, it's been a while since we played tennis. But there are two huge racquets that hit me, two huge shotguns, two billiard balls, in the world's court, horror, playing with us, playing with me.

It wasn't fire, and you said it well, no it wasn't fire. Someone started to call me. Come, he said. And I went. What do you need? he asked. I need some sleep. The clocks woke me. No, it wasn't the cold. No, it wasn't the game. I still have the clown's pants. I still have my pockets full of sand. I still open my arms and embrace you. No, it wasn't the game. I still don't have hatreds in the sand. I don't have knives in my pants. I have stars. Listen to me. My huge stars drawn in the port, the ships of my welcoming. My innocent farewells. The world won't leave me in peace. But the stars, the ships, the caramels, the soap bubbles, the centaur. No, it wasn't the game. I've looked through elevators, prison bars, handcuffs. And the world looks forever like a star to me. Its huge dungeon and its huge jail imprison me on the seashore. There is no exit, there is no outlet from the sky, only an echo screaming: I'm still living in the stars, I'm still sleeping in the stars, still. What do you need? he asked me. I need to sleep in the stars.

Mathematical equation, you said, the multiplication of bread and fish. A centaur's eye wanted to go through the mouse's needle. A really big man wanted to be a dwarf. But failed. Then the world marched onward. Wire boots, how could it be? Mathematical equation. The world declined twice. Life played a poor hand. Stood up furious. And moved far away from the city. Mathematical equation, they shouted, the multiplication of bread isn't going anywhere. I'm marching somewhere, said the soldier. Ha! Ha! Ha! Ha! An elephant's eye wanted to go through an elevator. The doormen stopped it. Ha! Ha! Ha! Ha! The world's bicycle, where is it? Ha! Ha! Ha! Ha! I don't have your underwear. It's not my fault if you can't find it, said life. And the world started laughing. Mathematical equation, you said, nothing is marching forward. The little dwarves didn't know what was marching, neither did I, I have to admit. The world is marching nowhere. Ha! Ha! Ha! Ha!

My tanks were filled with gasoline and wars. I was a lead soldier. I marched against the smoke of the city. There were difficult moments and there were, Hello! How are you? They were all worth the same. I had two pennies. I could enter the city. But they closed the doors on me. I closed my soul on them. They didn't know what had happened. Did my soul pass by here? Body, I said to you, how are you? I have been a lead soldier. The voice that said it was not what it said. I almost swear by the road. But the segment, the march loaded with clay, eyes of asphalt, hands of lime, legs of drill, navels of cement, resounded, resounded, resounded—the anvils of the hammer against the beams of the body—drilling, drilling, drilling me. Marching in time, the wall and the latch, the heart, my soul, the precipice of the trucks. And everything was black, black, black, white—like the asphalt. And the world closed its doors—anvils and hammers against the sleeping men—the doors of the heart, cities everywhere and little lead soldiers.

2. Poems of the World; or, The Book of Wisdom

Fool: *Nuncle, give me an egg, and I'll give thee two crowns.*
Lear: *What two crowns shall they be?*
Fool: *Why, after I have cut the egg i' th' middle and eat up the meat, the two crowns of the egg.*

—Shakespeare, *King Lear,* act 1, scene 4

I want everything to be in my book. So nothing is left unsaid. I want to say it all. Live it all. See it all. Make everything anew. The end must be the beginning. The exit from the tunnel. The entrance to the highway of life. The motorcycle chase. The full-moon gaze. I was the magician. All must know it. The world must know it. I was the only magician who performed a trick on a page. And the nightingale appeared. And the girl with red slippers. And the poet appeared. The poet. The poet. The barefoot poet. The child. The comet. The musicologist. I invented the treble clef. I invented the star of drama. So much time has gone by. I'll close my eyes. To be alone. Alone. Alone. I'm the loner. I would have liked to make you happy. I would have liked to invent paradise. An ice tavern. Or a milkman. A puppy. And a penguin. And I have it all. I have it all. I'll soon extinguish myself. Like a flash of lightning. Like the entire planet. Orchestra. Orchestra. Let the music begin. Let the singer begin to sing. Let everything begin anew. I want everything. Everything. Everything.

I hope your eyes never get tired of shining. I want it all. Eyes that shine like stars. Let me have stars in my hands. Let me draw comets for you. Let there be air and let there be earth. May you have what stars have. May they have what the sea has. May all have hands and comets. May all your wishes come true. May your hopes never stop waiting for you. May the star wait for you. May your wishes wait for you. May you be loved. May all love you. May you be filled with it all. May all fill you with innocent bagatelles.

I am the actor of hope. I am the dancing doll. I am the singer of the wind. I'll fly, I'll jump, I'll blow my golden trumpet. I'm inside—the feet, the head of the sea, the eyes of the wind. And I feel I'm going to fall at the exact moment when rivers contract. I invite you to dance for me, to laugh at me, to say yes to me. I am your dancer, your maiden, your sewing frame. I am the act and the word. I have nothing.

I don't have it, and I wanted it. I really, really wanted it, and I searched the water, the air, and the earth. And I walked and didn't give up. My eyes were frost. And my hands were long, and I waited so, so long I didn't give up. And I became so blind I didn't see it. And I searched and searched and didn't give up. I searched for it. I had it when I searched for it. And I wanted it when I didn't have it because I searched and searched. I had it, I had it when I didn't have it and searched and searched. My lips call it and it always comes asleep, sleepwalker, sleepless, and it's sleepy, sleepy, and it's sleepwalking when it listens to the wind, and it's asleep in the bare stockings of my torn shoe, and it mends my destiny and my sound and my way and fills me with light and wheat and harvests the wheat of my hands and tangles the ways and spins the winds and fills me with wind and wheat and sound and frost and pain and the hot and the cold of rivers and ways and winds and dreams, and it harvests my crops and heals my fruits in my bare stockings.

What joy. What joy. How happy you make me. How happy you've made me these days. What a thrill. What a high. What a trip. I'm so full of memories. The intensity of your body. The way we could love one another. The way we did love one another. What joy. What joy. How happy you've made me these days. What a great surprise. Really great. Pleasure so great. Really, really great. Thank you, love. Thank you. I can't bear so much pleasure of love and joy and passion and memories and gratitude that will issue to the north or the west of my bliss, and I can't find my way out of this bliss but I want to be inside it swarming with fireflies and wasps. What fun. Love. What fun. Love. What joy. What joy. How empty and how full of passion. And how full of bliss. Love. So full. Joy so full. And such passion, love. How full of joy and passion and pain and love and bliss. And how empty. How stuffed and how complete and how empty.

How empty and how full of joy. I won't describe you, I'll love you, I'll love you, above the sky, love, above all, you are there, love, with your love, you are there, love, you are there. And I want you to be above all, love, above all, so that all is under your love. All your love is there and is above all. Nothing exists without you above all. There is no *underneath*, there is no *in front of*, there is no *beside*. Only you, love, and you, above all, only you, and you, love, you, who are big and small, you, who buzz around like bees swarming and making honey from my beehive, and you, who stop in my heart. Inhabiting everything.

Everything inhabited and supplied by you. Nothing is empty. And you are empty and full, and you hunt me like a wild beast and tear my skin, and you are the hunter in my forest, and I am the gazelle and you the vulture, love, and I the tiger. And in the forest I am the star and firefly and you the cistern and I the cherry and you the walnut and I the almond. And you the deer and I the turtle and you the serpent and I the snail. And you happiness and you hope and I grief, love, over the forest and the jungle. You are there, love, with your shotgun and your lance and your crossbow and your arrow wounding my deer, love. And there is also the boar and the pig and the gazelle and the tiger's dance, and the love, above all the fairs and festivals and lotteries is your love, love, your love and your love. Above the forest and the feast and the jungle is your love. Love. Love. Love.

I love hiccups and I love sneezes and I love blinks and I love belches and I love gluttons. I love hair. I love bears. For me, the round. For me, the world. Round is the happy face. And round is the midday. And when the moon is most beautiful is when it's round. Sex is round. And the heart also. The hand is round. The mouth also. Sneezes are round. And hiccups also. The milk from the breast of Lady Macbeth was also round. I would have liked to be like her and be bad. I am good. I am Bacchus. I am sex. And I am hiccup. And I am sneeze. And I am cough. Hoarse. Hoarse. Hoarse. I am thunder. I am voice. I am obscene. Obscene. Obscene. I am pure like the tit or the milk. I am water, sea, or fish, or tadpole. I am round.

I'm so full of beetles and serpents, and I'm so full of ants and tadpoles and toads and snakes, and I'm so full of joys and lightning and stars. Don't say that we're so full, we're so empty and so full, someday I'll say and I'll repeat, of all the stars, and I'll return to the house of mirth. I'll burst and I'll work, work, work. I'll light a torch of happiness. I'll fill cauldrons and kettles with potions and pigs and toads. And I'll be the king of infinite space bounded in a nutshell. A little worm or a little ant, that snakelike thing that slithers. The outbreak of leprosy, the stench of the breed, and the plague, the mange. That's not to say, the breeze, the air, the morning. Happiness will blast off, a backlash of lighting. I'll create a work. I'll work. I'll work. I'll return to the house of mirth, I'll listen, jump, cheer. I'll answer, curse, wreck, ruin, rise charged with anger, fed up with the night, no, with round-trips. I'll make my way back, that's for sure. The rest of the sileni don't expect it, and I still don't know anything about it.

I'm so full of seven wonders. One is made of sun, another of snake. One is sand, another sea, another land. And another is the happy face, the joyful face. And the little worm. One is hen. Another duck. And another female or snail or male. Another youth. The old man and the boy. The water boy. The trumpeter. And the orchestra conductor. One is the Pied Piper of Hamelin. Another is well-being, pleasure, pain, orgy, silenus, faun. Another is love's wound. One could be my brother or my distant cousin. A surprise could be another. One is a loud buzzing buzzer. Waking up in the morning is another wonder. Wonder. Wonder. The orange vendor. Sleeping Beauty is another. And the alarm clock is the third. I'm missing five wonders. You could be the fifth. Maybe it's the black man on the corner. Or the tin drum. The fleeting chimera. The meowing black cat. The hen minding her chicks. I still don't have seven wonders. I'm missing the third or the fifth. I have the perfect match. There is a lonely wonder. The lamp goes out. There is a darkness that is a wonder. I'm missing the third. Missing the fourth or the sixth. All my wonders are joyful and content. I have them teeming with wonders. I'll abandon them, I'll burn them, I love them so much. They are happy and full. They are healthy and robust. They are wonderful. Wonders. Wonders. Wonders.

I have all surprises open. The gift was happiness. I can't hide it, open, open, all my doors open. I have no secrets to hide. A gift is a wonder. A slow sound in another wonder. Deafness of thunder. And blindness of lightning. And even my ear is wonderful. An orbit full of joy. An astronaut in the sea. Space of water is another wonder. And walking and traveling and greeting. And remembering and drawing and dreaming, a shell with its nut, or a grain of honey, sugar, and salt with the sea. But the return home, eve of the sea, sad tale of the idiot, poor cross-eyed girl at the corner. Green butterfly. Delayed hope. Day arriving dressed as yesterday. And the plaza in its flock. Gold, parrot, cricket, serpent, river, question, dwarf. Hall of mirrors, wild swans, answers, let's see if you're telling me the truth, you lied to me, I already forgot about it, you told me yes and it was no. No, it's not yet. Not yet. I will be born. I'll create a work. I'll work it. I'll make it. And I'll see it all.

The fruits are about to burst, about to provoke thunder, or a storm, or a root, or a sky. The day is about to burst. I'm about to give birth, about to have a pup. The sun is about to dawn. The moon is about to be full. The mother is about to suckle. The poet about to write. The man about to die. The shy about to speak. The deaf about to hear. War about to break. Peace about to return. Storm and thunder about to. Rainbow about to. And also memory about to. Sound about to. Living about to. Laughter about to. Well-being about to. Smile about to. Sickness about to. The killer about to kill. The dancer about to dance. The clown to cry. The child to scream. The conductor to conduct. The violinist to play. The audience to applaud. Love to erupt. The door to slam. The drum to beat. The plane to soar. The stork to deliver. The lion to roar. The poet about to write. About to die in peace. About to live in peace. About to be happy. About to scream. About to love. About to sleep. About to create and create and create and erupt and explode and scream and laugh and sleep and dream and laugh and create and create and give birth and have stars and thunder and lightning and pups. And about to groan, sleep, dream, scream, give birth. And create. Create. Create. Create. Create. About to create. Create. Create. About to dream. About to create, create, create, create.

The chestnut vendor looks like a nut. Looks like a tadpole, a toad, a mouse. She is scratching a nut. And feels a tickle. Feels an itch. She's got chicken pox. Measles. Leprosy. And a blue butterfly. Roaring thunder. The witch drops a piece of porcupine into the cauldron. There's a thorn at the tip of her nose. The orchestra explodes. And the ballerina fell in love with the killer. The hurricane fell in love with the thunder. The boy thinks he'll be a man. The trumpeter fell in love with his nose. He's nasal. Nasal. Nasal. The Pied Piper of Hamelin fell in love with the mouse. The Pied Piper is a magnet. The weight lifter has muscles that look like clouds. They're not clouds. They're muscles. They're thunder. They're nuts. The chestnut vendor wears an apron. The boy dresses like a tumbler. The bench feels lonely, lonely. The loner is full of chestnuts. The chestnut is a basket full of oranges. There is a seed in the fruit. A chestnut in the shell. The trumpeter blows the trumpet. The shell cracks open. The boy falls down. The ballerina dances the minuet. The violinist plays the wrong note. Hurricane, trumpet, thunder, orchestra...

The sweet madman and the bitter madman started laughing… I won't say what they were talking about, I don't even know. I relate to the mesh and the wand. Do I look like an idiot? I'm a tuna melt. I'm a cracked egg. I'm the same as you are. A pair of red slippers. Dance, I will dance. Idiot. Idiot. Your eyes are popping out. Your eyes shiver from the cold. My lips kissed, kissed, kissed. And they opened. And yours closed, closed. I have nothing more and nothing less. I shrug my shoulders, I don't give a damn. I'm indifferent. Indifference shuts like a tooth. And bites me when it shuts. I'm sad, worried, and helpless. You have to change the record. I know this melody by heart. Change, change the scenery. The sweet madman and the bitter madman started lamenting…

They don't recognize me. They don't know who I am. I'm sadly helpless. I was an earthworm, and a little dwarf, and I believed I was a giant, but I was a nut, and I was becoming an egg. They cracked my shell in halves. My yolk flowed. The yolk of my egg was yellow. They ate me. And I blazed, blazed. I am the yolk of the sun. I am a golden acorn. I am wheat. I am aniseed. I am hurricane and thunder too. I tremble with dread, I tremble with fear. I protect myself from the sun. Then I doubt, but I feel the water. I am the sweet madman. I am the bitter madman. I am helpless amidst thunder. The wind blew off my hood. I have an ant and a snail. And I sleep in a shell. I am the egg. I am the yolk. I am the cloud of the egg white. I am the nourishment. I am the leftovers. It is I. Be careful you don't throw me away. I might become an egg again and start blazing.

Stand up, sit down, jump, shout, slide, roll, yell. Curse, burst. Be a knave and a busybody. Be a fool. Be a rascal and a piece of cork. A fried egg. A rotten egg. A rotten orange. A snowball. A piece of porcupine. A soccer ball. A man. A man. He stood up and jumped. He looked like a ball. He looked like a fried egg. I shouted. Yelled. Screamed. Smashed. I was a tuna melt. A fried egg. I was the yolk of the sun. The roundest egg that ever existed on the roundest planet that ever existed. I have fingers. I have a mouth. Hands. Balls. I have a shirt and pants. I'm naked. Stand up and shout it. Walk. Stand up. And yell it. Walk. Run. I am. Man. Man. I am. The world. Leg. Life. Laugh. Smile. Tooth. Thigh. Leg. Mouth. Ear. Face. Nose. Navel. Laugh. Laugh. Face. Ear. Life. People. Man. Life.

I am the round heart of the ball of the world. And I am tired of being thrown around, as if my hand were worthless, as if my legs didn't know how to bounce back. I love so much. I make a vow. I throw the ball. It's only a game. A round game. Which takes my eyes. Leaves me blind. I don't believe it. I have a ball. And lots of other things. I have everything. I have it all. You have to believe me. I'm ready to corner it all. I'll breathe fire and fury. I'll get pregnant and love my belly. I love my belly inflated. And I love the exact moment of having pups. Then I groan. Then I bleed. Then my belly collapses. Then I'm the army ant. And most of all the kangaroo. How odd. What a weird feeling. It's pale. It's pale. But it's airy, bulky, and heavy too. And later the explosion. So the puppy whimpers. So the chick cracks his shell. I like fried eggs. I like shells. What would I do without this protective shell? That's why I love the acorn. It reminds me of a nutshell. And a nut is an aniseed. Such drunkenness. But I'm missing the yolk of the sun. And I'm unbridled. Where is the ostrich egg? It's playing hide and seek. Playing hide and seek, but the egg, that's it, the golden acorn, and the chimpanzee that I'm so in love with. And here is the result: the acorn, and from that giant chimpanzee grew the oak. And from the oak, the dwarf called by another name, man. What a fine thing to learn.

Let's see. Everything that is made up. Look at the busybody and the knave, at the cistern and the army ant. The ant's kingdom seems to me like a soccer player. And like a porcupine. And a cistern. The child who cannot heave her heart into her mouth. Explodes. Explodes in a different way. She has a cherry that looks like a heart. It's not a heart, of course. It doesn't listen, doesn't hide. It blasts. And blares. Like a trumpet. It makes a curious, queer sound. But what a jumbo ear. It looks like mine. I have an elephant's ear. And a dunce cap. I won't leave anything empty. There's a hole here. It's not deep, it's not a bucket, and it's not a well. There's a wound too. And it's not an ear. I spoke of the eye placed above my nose. And above is my forehead, and my hair too. The ear is a lie detector. The mouth is so big and so small. And what about the tongue. Even the ant has a tongue. And the little earthworm is red. No one walks as wrinkled as a caterpillar. It's a pity that a dancing serpent doesn't amount to much. I prefer a snake a thousand-fold because it has fangs. Sneaky dog. Just like a fox. Don't hide the flower. Be the hidden serpent. Stick out your tongue. Make a face at me. Porcupine. You rhinoceros. I have yet to meow. It's not enough to speak.

Everything keeps changing on us. Suddenly, a heart appears. I see it, watch it. And see it's not round. It has no blood. It has a pulse and a star. It has everything I want you to be. I want nothing, except what I want. And I want the heart of the boat. I like the boat because it's wide. Because both of us, the ant and the thunder, fit inside. Let lighting explode. And let an egg appear. And let the sunset spill over. It's the yolk, the yellowest part of the heart. It's thick. It's like a boat. It reminds me of a white cloud in the shape of an old man. It's like an old man in the shape of a star or lightning. It's a monkey, a chimpanzee. An acorn hiding a cloud. And the cloud will give birth to rain. And, of course, to the acorn and man. And man isn't a boat, isn't an oak, isn't sun or star or lightning. Although the white beard will always be a blue cloud and have stars, it will also be the blue beard or the rain, and when it rains it will never be lightning or thunder. It will suddenly be the heart.

Everything is yellow because everything is red because it has lightning and puppies and because it has a sky, a stork, and a penguin. Everything is black because it's yellow because the cloud bursts and because rain falls because you laugh and because you lust and groan and own a violin and a trumpet and a king and a crown and a prince and a courtier and a harlot and a bastard and a water boy and a tit and dick and a nose and a mouth and a tongue and a day and a ray of sunshine and a cold night and a rascal and a knave and a waif and a brat and a scrag and a goalie and a fried egg and a pygmy and a tapster and a preacher and a king and a smile and a happy face and a world full of joy. Everything is yellow and everything is noisy because it's silence and it's orgy and because it's lightning and morning and sunrise and fall and spring and summer and squall.

The world is a billiard ball. It's the egg and the yolk, and it's the reign of the pawn and the court of the king. The world is the courtier and the harlot and the bastard and the pygmy and the grasshopper and the butterfly and the river and the morning. This town crier and the mother with her puppy and the brewer and that town crier and one moment please and do-re-mi-fa-so and a chorus of ghosts and the song of the nightingale and the miss and the mister and yesterday and today and whatever lies ahead. And a fuckit and a dammit and a dwarf and a giant and a tit and a dick and a lip and a nose and an apple and a hand and a leg and two ears and my mouth and my tooth and tongue.

This is different. Here is a question. Here is a sky. An ostrich. A corpse. The world is round. Eyes are round. Round is the busybody, and round is the knave. Round is the ostrich egg. Round is the millet grain. Round is the soccer ball. Round is the sun's yolk. Round is the bastard's insult. Round is the brewer's malt. Round is the drunkard's tavern. Round is the waif, and round is the rascal too. Round is the whore. Man is so round, and so round is the sky that seems like a bunny and seems like a ball. Seems like a fried egg and seems like a dead dog barking at the infinite. It's an aniseed. It's the prophet of centuries, and it's the centaur too. It's a boy galloping on horseback. It's the king of infinite space. It's the round egg.

Eggs are months and days too. The roundest day is an egg. The tip of your nose looks like an egg. And mouth is egg. And tongues suck eggs. And balls too. And apples lay eggs. And seeds too. And roots are eggs. And seas too. The sky. The puppy. And the stepmother is an egg. Fried chicken is egg. And fire is egg. And what is rotten is egg. The plague plagues like eggs. And life tastes like eggs. A boy is an egg, a fried chicken. His mother is a hen. And his stepfather, a cock. If cock plus hen equals ostrich egg, then cock equals cuckold. And crest equals cock. The snail hides his head in an eggshell. I need a house like the head of a cock. I need a hood and a hut and a shack and a shanty and a shell where I can incubate all the eggs of the world. The world is a fried egg. And a rotten egg too. And it's yolk. And it's piss. And it's the world because it smells and lives within the egg and the day tastes like an egg and even a star is somewhat like an egg. And I am egg and always will be, and we are eggs and always will be. Fried eggs. Or rotten eggs. Boiled eggs. Or scrambled eggs. Poached eggs. Or round eggs. Eggs. Eggs. Eggs.

Listen how they fly, they seem, seem, they are, are, and they are not, and they are, are sexes and beings and they are, are the same, a bird, a thunder, a storm. And they are, look, there they are, in the sky, in the jungle, at home, on earth, in death, in life. And they fly and revive, they are born and they sleep, they awaken, with wings, and they walk and bark and growl, and they get angry and lose patience and make up, or they go and get drunk or look or laugh or walk. And they are frightened and furious, or they get undressed, and love, and sex, and sexes, and creatures and men and beasts and males and females. A sex, an adventure, and a monkey or a zebra, and a day or a bonfire, and a wound or a death.

The world is invaded by sexes and beings. The world is an orgy of pleasure. The world is robust and healthy, and fat, fat are the males and females, the zebras and ducks. Animals are pregnant with sexes, and women are milking their sexes and tits and breasts and bushes and springs and fountains and forests and groves and growls and meows and howls and bells and sex, and sex is trembling from pleasure and orgasm. Everything is orgasm and bacchanal and orgy. Ape and apple, rhinoceros and pear, jungle, crossbow, wild boar and unicorn, and trumpet, and rifle and ray and rainbow, and sea, and sun and moon, and the primitive dance of SEX.

The world is a blank. It's a slate or a chalk. It's a snake. Or it's the ostrich. Or the iguana. Or heaven. Or Mont Blanc. Or the sun that looks like a zebra. It's a great big Z. It's a giant giraffe. It's the word and it explodes. Bursts. It's not the mountain. It's not hope. There is an X that doesn't multiply. There is a zebra with stripes. (=), no, it isn't =. It's minus X or it's minus Zebra. And the Z is a hat. And there's a kangaroo that curses. A nasty word, really nasty. I prefer lies. To lie is to laugh. To curse is to spit. I feel the saliva. It's the zebra element multiplied in a swamp. It produces a panther. A Bengal tiger. Or a leopard. Yellow. Orange. Brown. Or white. Somewhat ferocious. Fierce means wrinkling your nose. And shockin'em. Shakin'em up. And laughing. And making faces. And scarin'em. Sticking out your tongue. Really long. A gag. A funny face. A sharpener.

The world is a dollhouse. A purse full of surprises. A lock. A prisoner. A princess. An animal. A savage cry. And a flower, or a mushroom. An aniseed. A brave, brave wave rises like a flock of sheep. And it's an army, and it's a war, and a cook, and a barber. It rises seething and mad like a poisonous snake, like a rabid sow, and it's a poor puppy or a calf. The cow looks like a tit. Muscles or veins are snakes or whales. The kangaroo is in a hurry. A hurry-scurry. The hyena's little kid looks like a flying ant. And the car stops. And the singer does her makeup and gets dressed. The policeman speaks. And the witch goes into the cauldron. She has many tails, many eyes, many ears, many noses. You stink like a slimy tadpole, you jackass, jerkoff, lizard. Don't insult him yet. We're at the beginning of the month. And we still have a year to go. Being born, that's as easy as laying an egg. The hard part is mating and growing.

I've just turned life into a proverb. I've just killed it. So that I may advise you. Mind your own business. Hatch eggs and bear pups. Hang out in bars and get drunk. Walk backward and you'll regret it, you'll really regret it. Don't stop at corners, stop midway. Men are better off when they're done with their booze and whores. Then they cry. And horses neigh. Dogs bark. And the moon vacations in Alaska. Snow is not white. A rainbow is blasphemy writ large. Twilights never last until dawn. Least of all today. There is an eclipse. The great bear left my city. I've just turned myself into a proverb with the stars. A meteor banished me from life. Beware. Night is falling. Be careful, walk on the shady side. A man is not a man until he makes ten mistakes. Then he starts walking and falls. He looks in a mirror and finds himself handsome. Then he discovers that he has ears. And listens. Sometimes he talks. Something worries him. And he knits his brows. Then he gets angry. And shouts. He goes on walking and doesn't arrive, doesn't arrive. He never arrives and returns. Life loves him. The sun warms him, burns him. Man yells. It's life. It's pain. Just a moment. Walk in the shade. Man was stitching hope. The green thread broke. Well, where is it? Did it show up? Where did it go? It's not my problem. I don't care. Don't hatch eggs. Get ready. Learn. Grow. Understand. Understand. And die.

This is the Child Mother of the circus and the earth and the penguin and the big snouts and the flowers and the child whose belly is full of earthworms and lizards and pigtails and lions and panthers and pandas and elephants. The Child Mother had such beautiful children. I bore the earth ten times and the sun twenty more. I bore knaves, barrels, and wine casks. I bore oil and vinegar. And I bore the hot and the cold. She grew like hens. And chirped liked baby birds. And was the ugly duckling. And was the black swan too. The Child Mother is giving birth. Out in the street. Throwing pots, pans, bowls, barrels, and junk on the ground. I throw everything on the ground. I want to feel the noise. I want to smash everything. Blow everything to smithereens. Detonate the machinery of the universe.

I bore it because I had to vomit it all. And I had to piss. I bore it on the ground, in the mud, with my fingernails filled with dirt. And I caught a whiff of urine, and felt that mud and dirt were inside my belly. And my belly button was a well and there was a huge cavern inside and a child walked naked amidst the storm. And I was naked and newly born. And I yelled—screamed and laughed and pissed and wailed. Then there was a wave of dirt. Everything was full of mud and everything was pure and had lice and ticks and bedbugs and middays and peaches and ashes. And peaches and moles were clay. And the bastard and the whore had slaps and had leopards and pomegranates. And I bore it. I wanted to bear it and my belly had ducks and hens. I didn't think I could bear it. That's why I puked. And spat. And screamed. And laughed. And slept. And rose. And I was thirsty. And needed bonfires. And needed diapers. And mothers. I had to bear it. And that's why I pissed. And danced. And gathered the shards of the world and threw them even harder against the ground, and heard them fall. And I exploded. Exploded. Exploded.

I haven't finished saying it, and I haven't finished living, or spitting, or pissing either. A knickknack could be full of me, but if it lacks some little tick or tack, it won't be a knickknack. And so the train moves on the rails of my clutter. And there aren't any diapers or kerchiefs that are umbrellas, that can suddenly stop a rainbow. And sometimes a fire kindles without the rubbing of two stones. And sometimes it starts without the striking of a match. And other times I find myself alone again, thinking. Never fall in love. Never cry. Piss. And burst. Look underneath the world. Look underneath things. Look at the surface of the lake. Look at the mirror and its reflection. And look at the sun. The meteor. The sky. The puppies. The moon. The she-duck. The he-goat. Wake up naked. Get dressed and undressed. And look. Look a lot. And drink a lot. And if you can fall asleep, sleep. And wake up. And forget it. Forget it. And remember it. And don't remember and don't forget it. And look at mountains too. And bark like a dog. And become a dog. And stork and snail and fire and keep things inside you, and keep the sun in mind, and the stars too, and the swings and the seesaws will help you go up and will help you go down too. And up and down.

After morning comes afternoon. And after that the sun sets. The sun sets. And night arrives. And there is a waning moon or a full moon. There are people too, males and females. There are penguins and wineskins and puppies and torrential rains and wise men and fools. There are books, and there are Psalms, and there are Proverbs. There are fishwives who shout. Shout. Shout. They sell dirty pots. And sell reheated soups. And there are wounds. And there are wars. And fireworks. And noises. And men sleep and work. And women sleep. And work. There are trades. Poet. Water boy. Lawyer. Doctor. There are carnivals. Ant there are holidays. There are duels. The duel of the viscount and the abbot. Of water and wine. Of salt and pepper. And of oil and vinegar. There is a river. And there is the bitter sea. And there is black grief. And Solitude is a character. And night is the color of mourning. And morning the color of happiness. And there are giraffes and skyscrapers. And loudspeakers and policemen and elephants. And every night an old man dies. And by dawn a puppy is born. And a grain of sun and an aniseed and a new century. And it so happens that Fridays end. And Saturdays arrive. And Sundays are for going with Papa to the merry-go-round.

I speak of the foolish world and the wise world. And I speak of its mountains and its lakes. I speak of its landscapes and its paintings. Of Rembrandt. Of Brueghel. And of Van Gogh. I also speak of Rimbaud. And of Shakespeare. And of Goethe. And of Dostoevsky and Lorca and Pound and Artaud. I speak of Plato's daimon. And I speak from Proverbs and Psalms and Prophesies. I speak from Nietzsche. And from Shakespeare. And I speak of the old man and the boy. And I speak from the grain of sun and from the grain of wheat. And I speak with beggars. With blind men. And with paralytics. And knaves. And jesters. And murderers. And monkeys. And chimpanzees. I speak with idiots. And wise men. And I speak with princes. And courtiers. And lawyers. And misanthropes. And I speak with Molière. And I speak with Rabelais. And I speak with food. In my mouth. And above all with banquets. And with the multiplication of bread and fish. And with astronauts. And horoscopes. And fame. And immortality. I speak with the moment. With my eyes open and with my eyes closed. And I always speak of life. And I always speak of death. And I always speak of the wheel of fortune. And I always speak of mankind. And I always speak of life.

I speak and will speak of the world. Of Leonardo da Vinci's circle of man. And I speak with Michelangelo's sculptures. And I speak of Beethoven and of Goya's black paintings. I speak of Picasso's blue period. And I speak of Guernica. And of the fat women of Rubens. And I speak of drink and of Dionysus and the fauns and the horns of plenty and the fat cows and the lean cows. From the Bible I choose the Book of Job. The Book of Psalms and the Proverbs. And of the wise men I choose Solomon. And of the prostitutes I choose the whore who sells herself on street corners. And I speak of knaves and of King Lear's fool. I speak of the egg. And of life. I speak of love. And I speak of kindness. And of evil. And I speak of Mephistopheles. And of Satan. And of earthly hell. And of pantheists. And of Deists. And of the Holy Trinity. And of trilogies. And of twins. And of belly buttons. And of earthworms. And of Lombardy. And of hotheads. And of bellies. And of pandas. And of bedbugs. And of roaches. And of human misery. And of human comedy. And of tragedy. And of epics. And of heroes. And of those who died in war. And of tailors. And of boilers. And of nurses. Of cancer, leprosy, and the plague. And of disease. And of death. And of life.

It's not this or that. But I can't explain it. Here is the boy with curly hair. Golden locks. With red eyes. And red lips. Small feet. Bare slippers. The minuet. Harlequins, the trumpeter and his nose. Barrels in the wine cellar. Gray sky. The seagull looks like an earthworm. It moves and moves, the sky moves. It moves and moves, the sea moves. It moves and moves, the boy moves. Planes move. Castanets too. And chestnuts crack open. The knave insults the busybody. Just a moment, please. I am the drunkard. What the hell do I care. The bartender looks at him while serving him a beer. It's the tavern. It's the dollhouse. It's the world. It moves and moves, the world moves. Where is the exit? Where the bridge? Where the highway? Where the port? Where the seagull? Where the car? Where the music? I the boy with golden locks. I the telescope lens. I the looking glass. I the EXIT. I the silence. I the outlet. I the door. I death. Wake up. Wake up. It's late. Wake up. The train. The railroad station. Life. Death. The driver. The road. The river. The bicycle. Death. Life.

The world is an idiot, a box of broken teeth, and my molar that aches so, so much, the cripple cried, and ran, the tide of the wine cask ran. I'm the horn of plenty. Look at my shorts. Your mitt is lovely. It doesn't kill flies. But it does scare them away. There is a musketeer. But where are the other two? King Lear moans, moans, moans. The sun will come out amidst the storm. There must be a light, something that brightens it up. No, no, no, no, why should a fly have life. And you, Cordelia, no breath at all. What happened? The lion ate the mice. And the cat went wild. And the child who walked naked amidst the storm moaned. It's grief. The procession. The carnival. It's a concert. An orchestra. A fire. It's the Apocalypse of the Proverbs. It's the Psalm. It's the Book of Job. Without a beginning. There's an intermission. No, and no, and no. It can't be. Yes, it is. It can't be. She is dead. Dead. Dead. Cried King Lear. King Lear cried. Cried. Cried. Blind. Blind. Blind. Amidst the storm. Amidst the trumpet. Of the jubilation. Of the court. Of the world. Of the sovereign. Of the powerful. Of this tragedy. He cried. King Lear cried. Cried. Cried. Dead. Dead. Dead.

This is not a book. I did not read it. I lived it. I lived it from road to road. I came across the fortune-teller on the way. And the magician too. And I found a door closed. And gates. And guards. And cowards and killers. And street spectacles. And New York City. And the moon. And the sun. And thunder. And love. And death. And trains. And visionaries. And war. And the atomic bomb. And I found my ears. And I found my soul. My self. My poet. My stars. My comets. And I wrote. And I got drunk. And I loved. Loved most of all the mills and lions of Cervantes. And I loved César Vallejo. And I lived in Paris, Rome, and Madrid. And I locked myself in a room to write. And I also ate. And I was hungry and cold. And I fell in love. And forgot. And I'm ready to do it again. And I'm determined to finish this book with another life. With another affirmation of life. With another great, big Yes. Throwing junk on the ground again. And exploding. Let it explode. Yell. Jump. Let them out. Let them out of these pages. Let them get drunk. Let them love. Live. Sleep. And love. And rot too. And above all, die.

3. Pastoral; or, The Inquisition of Memories

All the world's a stage,
And all the men and women merely players.
They have their exits and their entrances,
And one man in his time plays many parts,
His acts being seven ages.

—Shakespeare, *As You Like It*

Just a moment, please. If you wish, ladies and gentlemen. And shepherds and shepherdesses. If you wish, idiots and drunkards and buffoons, to laugh or lament, it's worth your while to buy me. My name is Giannina. If you wish to sneeze or blink. Or if you wish to feel happy. Or if you wish to whistle. Or if you wish to see a show. Or play gin or poker. Or get drunk or cry. Read *Profane Comedy*. If you wish to become shepherds. And true shepherds. If you wish to find your way. Or if you wish to get lost. Or if you wish to return home. And find your soul. Read *Pastoral* of *Profane Comedy*. If you wish to complicate your life. And if you wish to calm down. Read me. Read me. Love me. Love me. If you still believe in childhood. If you're still five years old. Or if you have grown up. And you still have dreams and hopes. Call me by name. Call me Giannina. My phone number is 5-4-3-2-1. My address is New York. This is an ad. An ad turned into a book. A book turned into a character. Like the quenepa. And the nispero. Like the soul. Like the dream.

5-4-3-2-1. Hello! Hello! Giannina. Yes, it's me. Who is speaking? Hello! Hello! Yes, it's me. Giannina. And I'm furious. How dare you mention my name in the ad for *Profane Comedy*? And to give my phone number. I am already speaking to lawyers. You are facing a lawsuit. You have used me. Now just a minute, Giannina. Listen, what will my colleagues say? What will clowns, buffoons, and drunkards say? Let them say whatever they please. You and I know very well that you are not Giannina. You are Giannina. You are a fortune-teller. You are a drunkard. You are a buffoon. You are not Giannina. You are a shepherd.

Now I wish to speak to you from the bottom of my soul. I wish to speak to you of water jugs. And shepherds. I wish to speak to you of pipes and flutes. And flocks. And the gathering of sheep in my soul. I wish to speak to you of fountains. And wells. And water. There is so much water in the world. And there are so many meadows and valleys. And so many forts. And frontiers. I wish to speak to you of the lover. And his lover. And the question put to creatures. And green pastures. And pomegranate juice. And countrysides. And mountain. And the wine cellar. And the bed of lions. And the flowers of St. Francis. I wish to return home. I wish to arrive at the dwelling of my soul. And I wish to raise the diapers of dawn. And I wish to return to every sunrise. To turn on the lights. So they shine. And fountains return to water. There is a maiden. And there is a deer. And a stag. And morning is rising. And shepherds are leaving at the break of day. And night shepherds are singing. And baby birds are singing. Nightingales are singing. And snails are singing. And there is sea. And land. And mountain. Now I wish to speak to you at the break of day.

I just got up. Just after the break of day. When the sun starts burning the memories of the hours. When hours have ceased existing. When there is no time. When seasons no longer follow one another. When there is no spring or hell or heaven. When it's night and when it's still day. When it's day and already night. And it's three a.m. I am pure. I am a splash of light. I am lifting the ball of the sun. I am dawning with light. I am full of fire and heat. I am alone. Light is the edge of water. The frontier of day. There are beasts pissing on the beach. There are socks splashed with water. There is a white shore. And a ball of fire playing with the shore. There is a naked boy swimming in the water. There is a violet sunset streaked with silver. There is a jagged rock. There is a cavern of hermit crabs. And some tracks. And some shoes. Red ones.

I am the shepherd of water. The shepherd boy of dawn. I have a golden beetle. And I have a snail. Oh woe, woe's me! Music has invaded my beaches. Flooded my banks. Surrounded all my infinities with water. My sheep have run off. Have fled from the flock. Have left the earthquake of my home. And left me alone. Left me painted in the landscape of memories. But I have returned to my soul. Barefoot and hidden. Like a duende I have returned. Like an elf I have returned. Running. Fleeing. From the lie of love and memory. In the vineyard. In the wine cellar of the river. In the bottle of wine. Devouring nuts and collecting cards and stamps and albums. And dreaming. And remembering. And gathering seeds. And crossing forts and frontiers. Besieging time, which is Shepherd and Shepherd and Shepherd. And melancholy. Melancholy. Melancholy. And memories are. Still. Still. Still. I was shipwrecked. But I saved myself. And I sang epigrams and eclogues and odes and sonnets. And I'm still singing to sirens. And hearing their song. And writing the symphony of water. Of earthquake. Of storm. Of peace. My hell. My shepherd. My torture. My treasure. My sun. My sun. My do-re-mi. And my fa. And my soul. And my love.

On the top floor of the Empire State a shepherd has stood up to sing and dance. What a wonderful thing. That New York City has been invaded by so many shepherds. That work has stopped and there is only singing and dancing. And that the newspapers—the *New York Times*, in headlines, and the *Daily News*—call out: New York. New York. New York. Listen to it. Hear it on the radio. And on television. Listen to the loudspeakers. Listen to it. The buffoons have died. And the little lead soldier. Shepherds have invaded New York. They have conquered New York. They have colonized New York. The special of the day in New York's most expensive restaurant is golden acorn. It's an egg. It's an apple. It's a bird. Fish. Melody. Poetry. And epigram. Now there is only song. Now there is only dance. Now we do whatever we please. Whatever we please. Whatever we damn well please.

I'm really sorry, folks, but the shepherds are also farting in New York. I'm sorry. But they're disgusting. And the cops are pigs too. And they're farting too. And they're competing to see who can fart the loudest. So there's fart traffic. And burps. Traffic of bulls and cows and ambrosia and water. And bulls are pissing on buildings. And cows are shitting in shops. And all the shops are filled with shepherds. And all the mannequins are shepherds. I'm really sorry, folks, but the shepherds are disgusting. Filth. Filth. Everything is filthy. Everything is disgusting. Everything is full of caca. Cow caca. Worm caca. Lizard caca. Santa Claus caca. Vulture caca. Beetle caca. The streets are full of caca. And the food too. I'm sorry, folks, but New York is a filthy pig. A filthy, stinking pig.

I just got back from a trip to New York. I just got home. And I have seen the greatest thing. The finest thing on earth. I have seen the eyes of the most beautiful city in the world. I have seen the eyes of my city. I saw her sleeping. I was so shocked I didn't know what to do. I ran off in a panic through the streets. I got to St. Patrick's Cathedral and rang the bells. I have seen the eyes of my city with my own eyes. I ran all the way to the Empire State, went up to the top floor, grabbed a loudspeaker, and yelled to the people of New York City. I have seen with my own eyes the finest city in the world. I have seen the city I love. What should I do? What should I do? Except run. Run until I'm tired of running. Until I'm tired of running and running and running. And now she is getting closer. And closer. And I feel the eyes of my city. And I feel she's still near. I have seen the eyes of my city with my own eyes.

What'll I do in this traffic of shepherds? I'll blow my horn. I'll carry a whip and lash my cows. They can't get enough of grazing in the sidewalks. Can't get enough of mooing in the newspapers. Can't get enough of shitting. They're grazing dreams in the middle of New York. In the middle of the sidewalk. Muttering and screaming. Damn you all. Go to hell. Every last one of you. I'm in the hurricane of New York Airport. To hell with the suitcases. And taxis. Damn the soul. Bodies. And hearts. And groans. Damn the seeds. And roots. And passports. Get the hell away from me. Let me graze poems and sonnets with my shepherds. Airplanes and airports, leave me alone. I have a cow. I have a flute. I create this *Pastoral.* Damn it. And you can go to hell. Every last one of you, damn it. To hell with you all.

Adoration. Veneration. Exclamation. All the children were gaping. Mama. I like the whistle. Buy me a whistle. I want a whistle. Mama. I don't like this whistle. Mama. It doesn't chirp like a birdie. Mama. I want a horn. Don't you see I'm sad. Don't you see the clouds. Don't you see I want the sun. Mama. This whistle doesn't work. Mama. What junk. Why don't you buy me a whistle. Mama. I want another whistle. Buy me that one. That one. I don't want it anymore. What junk. Mama. You're a piece of junk. You look like a whistle. I want to get out of here. I'm fed up with hearing your whistle. Mama. I don't like your whistle. You're a nag. You look like a whistle. Get away. Mama. Look, your belly grew. And now you're ugly. You look like a whistle. And you don't know how to whistle.

I forgot to tell you something really important. I'm forgetful. And sometimes I'm lost. But I still have my eyes. And I still have my legs. And I don't know what to do with so many eyes and so many legs. It is a never-ending tale. The concert ends. And the poem begins. Food runs out. And I'm still hungry. I just got up. And I'm still sleepy. And when I return I wish to be where I was. We already know this stuff. It's a public affair. That's why I still feel like thinking. And dreaming. And laughing. And crying. I am always back again and beginning anew. I told you before, I am an egg. And now that I am shaking I know everything is different. And I don't want to return. Now that I'm about to come to the climax. Now that I'm made of mere tensions and mere tendons and pure dreams and pure color movies. Go ahead. Go ahead. The red light turns yellow and green. And from winters you subtract autumn and you add spring. And we are back in summer. It's weird. I swear, everything seems so strange. And the weirdest part is that everything seems so weird to me. What do I know. That we are lightning. That we are only flashes of lightning. That later everything will be one more crayon in the infinite frame of lightning, painted and finished.

I could be awake or dreaming. We all could be. But everything has to do with everything. And see you soon. A cloud so red. Lightning so square. So profound. So ambiguous. It must have been an airport. Or a concert. Or a dinner. Or a theater. Maybe it was a fried egg. Or a raven. Or a vulture. Or a mystery. Or a secret. Maybe I was still groggy. But Giannina was mute. But Giannina was blind. But Giannina was an idiot. But Giannina was a beggar. And walked filthy from the streets and mud. Filthy from having gone through the world. And from having smelled all possible smells. The first thing I ask is that you open your eyes. The second is that you see. That you walk. That you run. And that you see. You'll experience things you've never dreamed of. When you've returned from the other side of the world. When you've seen the light. When you've turned your back on sadness. I have planted poems in the saddest of the earth. I have painted Van Gogh. And I have been Zarathustra. I have descended the stairs. The sky is still far away. The sky is the seed. And the tree its harvest. And its history, the history of the stars. What could the infinite be. Stretch out your hand, blind, blind, blind. Stretch out your arms, Giannina. There's something about it that still falls short. That still calls me. And reaches me. And seizes me. What can morning be? Or hope? What can it have? What does it have? And what will it have? And what did it have?

Set your mind at ease. Breathe. And set the world on fire. So the whole city burns down. So all is created. Make yourself at ease, Giannina. Make yourself at home. In your memory. Don't burn its silence. Or the door. Go beyond the brink. And watch out. Sound out. Search. But don't make its life miserable. Don't take away its smile. Don't take its mouth. Or its word. Don't take its hat. Or its coat-rack. Don't take its purse, its shadow or mystery. Let it have a bite in peace. Let it take a nap in peace. So it doesn't have to burst. It already burst. Now it must relax. Every day off. Every holiday. Every day I do whatever I damn well please. Then the pinch. Or the tickle. Or the very chickpea that bursts. Or the very explosion that melts down. And goes home. As always. And opens its eyes. And sees. Sees everything. Retains everything. Focuses everything. Calm down, Giannina. Make yourself at ease on your rug. Your night spot. Your beehive. Let the watchman of the eye awaken from sleep. Awaken from death. Let him give the manuscript back to the earth. And let his mother in a carriage give back her son. And raise the earth. Nourish it. Amuse it. Entertain it. And leave it in peace. In peace until death. Leave it in front of the sea. Let it come face to face with itself. Without having to tell the truth. Without having to lie. Let it, let it, let it, finally live in peace. Let it. Let it die in peace.

I make the affirmation. I make the exclamation. I am the inquisition of memories. And I am bored by semicolons. I am bored by doubt. And above all, by memory. I am bored by memories and have reached the top of the world to burn them. My memories are in this book. Listen to me, ladies and gentlemen. This is the funeral of memories. This is their cemetery. This is their service. I don't worship them or respect them in any way. They belong to no one. They don't belong to the grave. They don't even belong to memory. You've all seen the red chimeras and the black chimeras. And you've seen the drunkenness and the banquets. And then the remains of memories came and cleared away life. Death is called memory. And so is time. And so are the damned garbage collectors. I mean the shepherds of memory. And memories are shadows. And memories are death. I am not a memory. I am not an arsenal of epithets or metaphors. I am the star, and the star shines. I am affirmation. And I do not want concepts. I do not want abstractions. No, no, no, and no. I am not a semicolon. I want a period and a paragraph. I want to end it all, once and for all. Without any regrets. Without memory.

Listen to me, ladies and gentlemen. Listen to the sermon of memories and sorrows. Listen to hell. Why didn't I do what I should have done. I repent. I have sinned. I have memories. And torments. I am burning in the flames of memories. Why didn't I keep quiet? Why did I do that? I repent a thousand times. Why did I betray you, and why do I remember you? Oh woe, woe's me! Oh, and I left you standing in the street. Listen to memories. Listen to them again. Why did I betray you? Why did you leave and forget me? And I grieve and remember you. And the worst were my tears. And the worst was remembering you. Listen to the soap opera and listen to memory. Oh! Now what's left for me! Just monologues, soliloquies, and memories. I'm left with shadows. I'm left with memories. I don't want monologues or sorrows or soliloquies. I am a singing bird. I am a child. I am the nightingale. What does winter or autumn or spring or summer know of memory? They know nothing of memory. They know that seasons pass and return. They know that they are seasons. That they are time. And they know how to affirm themselves. And they know how to impose themselves. And they know how to maintain themselves. What does autumn know of summer? What sorrows do seasons have? None hate. None love. They just pass.

Sermon of memories and sorrows. Sermon of everything negative. Sermon against senechism and hedonism. Sermon in favor of Bacchus and Faustus. Affirmation of the horror of the void. Of the horror of memories. And of the horror of silence. And the panic I feel every time I hear that all my memories have died. And I walk through the streets of New York alone. Without memories. And Giannina has burned the memories of the world. Burned the books of memories. Burned their mediocrity. Burned their memories. Burned their negations. So everything is said. So everything is said. So nothing is left inside. So spirit doesn't surpass matter. So summer doesn't outdo autumn. So nostalgia becomes impossible. Burial of melancholy. Poor thing. It died on Third Street. And I didn't care. I didn't grieve. Oh, woe, woe's me! Memories died. And I'm not mourning them. And I am a shepherd. How strange. This is the first shepherd that isn't grieving. Listen to her. She is a shepherd. And she is happy that her memories die. Happy that grief dies. Happy. Happy. And feels as happy as bells and stars. And she is a shepherd. And feels absolutely no grief at all.

Memories walk around dressed up as old men. But they're not old. They're hypocrites and gossipers. I love gossip. But I hate memories and sorrows. I like—he told me and I told him, and we fell in love, and rode off into the sunset, and lived happily ever after. I like the sun and the beach. I like sidewalks. And soup and beets. I like men and women. And I like mountains and seas. I like fire and water. I like trashy movies and novels. I like tackiness and gossip. Most of all, I like to forget everything. Especially memories. I am forgetfulness. And nothingness. I am joy, well-being, and happiness. I am laughter, gossip, and pantomime. I am the idiot and the prince. I am the grain of rice and the bean. I am the chickpea and the casserole. I am the red apple. And salt and pepper. I am the shepherd of life. I am the shepherd of memories, which I love despite everything. Affirming is everything I love and everything I hate. Affirming. And living. And denying. Affirming everything.

I am Giannina. And now it's my turn to rock and to affirm movement. As I affirmed the denial of memories. But what I deny is as powerful as what I affirm. Power is in my flesh. In my life. In speaking as I want and feel. I like to expect a lot. I do expect a lot. There are many ways of expecting. An ad is expected. Dinner is expected. Christmas is expected. Santa Claus is expected. Death is expected. Love is expected. The weekend is expected. A party is expected. Night is expected. Spring is expected. A baby is expected. A trip is expected. News is expected. Forgetfulness is expected. An invitation is expected. Hope is expected. Memories are not expected. They just come. Old age is not expected. It comes. Not death. It always comes. Not memory. It always comes. Not love. It always comes. Not forgetfulness. It always comes. Not children. They always come. Not happiness. It always comes. Not friends. They always come. Not memory. It always comes. Not Giannina. Always. Always. And now it's my turn to rock from side to side.

And now. If you see a shepherd of medium build. Small. With brown eyes gazing at the stars. Who has a smile on her lips. And perfect ears. Who wears a beret. Or a sailor's hat. If you see her walking with red slippers. If you hear jingle bells. If you see that she has rosy cheeks. And if you see that she has dimples. If you see that she looks at you and doesn't stop staring. If you see that she smiles. And greets you. If you see that she doesn't get tired of walking and dreaming. If you see that she gazes at the sky and the clouds and the stars. If you feel good and fall in love with her when you meet her. If you don't leave her alone. If you touch her. And touch her. And touch her. And take off her cap. And her red vest. And lie beside her. And speak to her. And you're surprised that she knows so much without knowing anything. And that she is so profound without being profound at all. And that she understands everything without understanding anything. And that she is the most famous shepherd in the world without having any fame at all.

The damned newspapermen are here again. What do you want now? Tell me. What do you want from me? We would like to know if drunkards, buffoons, and madmen collaborated with you, Giannina. We would like to know if you have already understood the meaning of the shepherds. We would like to know the difference between being called Giannina and being called a clown. We wish to know if you, Giannina, were at the banquet. And if you were the one who laughed and cried at the time. Tell us, Shepherd Giannina, what difference is there between a purple sunset and an orange one? What difference is there between the moon and the sun? Between being a drunkard and a shepherd? How many years did it take you to write the book? Why do you talk so much about shepherds? Who was the first astronaut who stepped on the moon? You also mention the batting of eyelids. And why did you leave the eyebrows out? Why didn't you paint the lips of the buffoons? Why did the fortune-teller read the past and not the present? What was the sky, and what was the night, and what was the day? Who were the porters? Why were the doors closed? What produced the orgy? And why are there more than five eggs? Why the newspapermen? And why the shepherds? Why a book like this, Shepherd Giannina? Why?

4. Song of Nothingness

The child is innocence and forgetting, a new beginning, a game, a self-propelled wheel, a first movement, a sacred "Yes."

—Nietzsche, *Thus Spoke Zarathustra*

Here. Astride the top of nothingness, I suddenly receive the call of death. Who, in passing, tells me that it's nothing. Nothing more than the absence of the word itself. Nothing more, and simply nothingness. Buds or roses. Lilies. Or emeralds. Smiles. Or teeth. Biscuits. Or birthdays. Visits. Or gatherings. Friends. Or acquaintances. Men. Or children. Old people. Or passersby. Bicycles. Or carriages. Airplanes. Or elevators. Tricycles. Or stairs. Stores. Or display windows. Clubs. Or coffee shops. Places that have just pulled away. Or faraway places. Absentees. They are all being eliminated. They are all testifying to the song of nothingness. To the song of forgetfulness. To the very return of nothingness. To my taking a step down. And I'll take another step down. And another. Until I reach the floor. To the very door of my exit. To the very tunnel of the womb. Or death. Or tomb. Or nothing.

Nothing. Everything looks like nothing. Everything is pale. White. Nothing. Everything is rotten. Everything is absurd. Nothing. Because everything is so difficult. Or because everything is so simple. Or because the world turns. Nothing. A television. A telegram. A concert. Skinny, emaciated poetry. A pale, thin poem. A sickly poem. As if the gasoline were running out. As if the fighter no longer wanted to fight. As if he were exhausted. As if his eyes were closing. As if he couldn't go on. As if he were about to drop dead. Over the tomb. Dead. As if poetry were ending. As if it had to end. As if the poet did not exist. He doesn't exist. It's reason enough for him to be quiet. Silence is suddenly born. The spokesman for death is born. What is born is always born. But nothing is here on top. Placing silences on things. Giving them moments of closure. Of enclosure. Giving them spaces or ways. Slowly. Walking with a child's bicycle. On a street. Someone passing by a building. By a building erected by silence. Or a void. Which will also become void. Even absence has its motives. And its hovels, its details. Its voids. One would suppose that at the end of so many details something must be found. But absence places a period at its beginning. Dots its silence. The absence of death. The absence of silence. The absence of exclamations and interjections. The absence of absence. Nothing.

I will speak of my absences. Of all my absences and my negligence on top of heaps of faults. On top of mountainous heaps or hopes. One bunny has two boy bunnies and a girl bunny. The same is true of squirrels. They multiply. And then they trample over us, men and more men. Women and more women. Absences and more absences. Three or four were missing from death or from life. They returned. Returned. One returns returning from life or from death. From the wheel that turns. From childhood one still returns. Down the stairs. The travelers returned. Returning from childhood. Or from abroad. Returning down the stairs or the elevator. One looks back. Looks back. Back. And writes a period. Doesn't write it. Feels absence imposed. Feels returned from absence. And feels it. It is felt without meaning. Without meaning or significance. I won't call him man. I won't call her woman. I won't be able to tell those who still haven't returned. But it must be felt. It must be lived. From the back. The back of life. The absence of life. She who went and did not return. She who went, never to return. It wasn't thunder or rain. It wasn't morning or afternoon. And it wasn't night. Or spring. It wasn't life. Or death. It was nothing less. Nothing more than nothingness. The nothingness that does not speak. That does not say a word. The nothingness that does not drown though it cannot swim. Nothing was the absence of nothing. Nothing was the nothing of absence. Absence was the nothing of nothing. It was the very nothing of nothingness itself. Absence.

Absence without wanting it. Without imposing its mandate, its power, or its sovereignty. It imposes its rule. It imposes its destiny. It imposes what must be imposed. Without there being lightning or thunder. Without there being a moment later. Neither forever. Nor goodbye. Just because it wants to be the same lost innocence. Just because of its remoteness. Or my distance. Nothingness just isn't. Isn't here. Unless it lay down to sleep on the core of its own void. On the tomb of its own vacuum. But the scream of nothingness would cry out even over this tomb. The testimony of the tomb or the nothingness would start to manifest itself. My voice would cry out over this nothingness that imposes its silences. Its deserts. Deserts of dust. Deserts of lives. Of winters. Of suns. Of silences. The screaming of nothing sets in. The breathing of death sets in. It imposes its corpse. Its distance. It imposes the testimony of nothingness. It imposes silences, suicides, the sad coming of dawn. It imposes rosaries. Upon the very tomb of nothingness.

I am a void that abhors the void. There is no possible explanation. Abhors it. And enough. Affirms. Walks and continues. Requests. Implores. Entreats. Sobs. Or cries. But abhors. Many moments of life have already been requested. And now I kneel. To implore. Sick. Only to ask. Only to beg. If it's possible. A moment. Only a moment to cry. Kneeling. And only a heart, only a memory, only a repetition. If it were possible, I'd want them to forgive me. A damned forgiveness. I don't want to ask for it or beg for it. A possible history. A possible repetition. And I'm fed up. And I ask my partner to dance again. Dance. Dance. I dance. And dance. Tip. Tap. Tip. Tap. Jig. Jag. Jig. Jag. Come here, gag. Asleep. I dream. Violent. I implore. And laaa. Leee. Laaa. Leee. Laaa. Violins. And trumpets. Bee. Bop. Bee. Bop. What's that I see? A mouse on the floor. What's that I see? An ant on the floor. What's that I see? Two little roaches in love with the floor. Or with life. Or with lightning. Or with thunder. Or with the wheel that turns and turns and turns throughout the universe turning around again. All over again. Click. Clack. Click. Clack. More. More. More. More. Two more times. Three more times. Ten more times. Fourteen more times. A dozen more times. Two hundred thousand more times. And more. And more. And click. Click. Click. Clack.

How many horrible things can happen to a man before. Or after. And it all hinges on beauty. Or the wheel. The climax is a navel or a stone. I stop and think. And maybe I'll throw a dart or a stone. I'm tired of watching. I'll penetrate now. I'll enter later. It's not the same exact spot. It's been two days. Two whole nights. Finished. Examined from top to bottom. Ten days of exhaustion. One long live joy. Or long live exhaustion. One more kilometer. You again. Me again. Behind the same pulpit. In the same classroom. A teacher. Dictating an invented destiny. A new word. Vocabulary. A closed book. Against this flower. Against this very flower. Against this very squirrel. Against the sun. Against all kinds of parachutes. Against the same ground. Against the same cold panther. Against the same dust. Crossed. Dust. Dust. Or fog. Smoke. Fires. Or flashes. That's to say. Let's give ten examples. Let's set our goals. Let's conjugate ten verbs. Let's eliminate them from the grammatical system. Let's take away their action. Let's invite them to a hypothetical grammatical time. Oh, moon, oh, star, oh life! And let's give them a chance to think. Behind a desk. Smoke, wind, dust. Above my eyes, two stars shine. Under my legs, face down, two lines meet that cross the same crossword puzzle. Without thinking, the solution is obvious. And still unanswerable.

A little while longer. Ten days repeated. I'm looking at the moon. The highest star. The solution to the same math problem. On a pile of conjectures. Polysynchronized colors. And the answer ten kilometers from my house. Proof for a theorem. I'll supply you with all the necessary material. I'll give you a certificate. A science diploma. Some goggles. From the time before iguanas and the world. A frog croaks. A cricket sings. I love bird nests. From the time before life. I love from dreams. Toad interpretations. I come whenever I hear iguana concerts. My orgasm is an organ. An organism. A simple tadpole that becomes a frog. A mouse has his own way of fighting a cat. He takes him out of context. The cat's text meows. Mice want cheese. Cows eat lots of meat. Polychromatic urban cows. Green. Orange. Or yellow. The piano, softly. Or the C in E flat. In A minor. Still listening to the symphony. Still. Allegretto. Fugue. Scherzo. Or andante con moto, or andante con brio, or rondo burlesco. In the rondo of the minuet or the waltz. A C in E-flat. Ten days of fugue. Music vacations. An ironic fit of laughter still rules over the sea. And a stupid drool.

This is not it, says the teacher. Not my child, says the mother. Nor has this tale ended. Ten more times. The same season of the year, says the old man. And he imagines a flower, said the painter of the world. Said the murderer himself. The leech, the bloodsucker. His tongue is red. Blood red. It's got red candy, said the boy. Days are better at the beach, said the swimmer. I'm naked, said the metaphorical man. The imaginary one drinks water. Thinks cognac. Thinks whiskey. Thinks scotch. Women always paint their nails the day before, said the manicurist. I'm in the world too, adds the polemicist. Polemics. I pretend I'm nearsighted. I'm a lefty, said the righty. The heart rests on the right side, said the nitwit. Two lines beside a great big X, said the mathematician. An experiment is a sin, agreed the scientist. I add—two experiments. I underline—a hypothetical exit. The labyrinth, said the minotaur. Or the museum, said the musician. Two notes simply rhyme, said the painter. And a locomotive appears, adds the metaphorical mechanic. So I won't be told that I'm not a poet, adds the novelist, underlining poet. Here is something special. Here is a gift. Here is a box. Here are the metaphors for all theories. Here is a new doctrine on how to begin.

Let's begin all over again. Let's begin by affirming that poetry has died. And that I'm not a poet. And I'll never, ever be one. I'm not interested in poetry. I don't like life. I detest men. I hate children. I hate the sea. I hate my mother and my father. I have no brothers. I have no family. Mankind disgusts me. I am bitter. My brows are knit, and I feel such envy. Such envy that resembles hope. That waits for others to die. I don't expect to die. I expect to kill you. I expect to devour you. I expect to destroy you when you least expect it. I'll drive ten knives into your back. And I'll turn saint. I will have killed what was the best in you. And I'll be happy. Happy you're dead. How I wish you were dead. Bastard. All these are my desires. But I won't confess them. I'll keep them close at heart. I am so good. So good. So good. I will live. I will live forever. I am the best of men. The most envious. The lewdest. The biggest pervert. The biggest liar. The most jealous. And the ugliest. I am the devil. The best angel in the world.

How can the music be playing so loudly? My ears are splitting. I can't stand it. It's not Beethoven. The absolute is too much. And so is the void. Dance and dance. Like a mouse. Or a small squirrel. Drink and drink, like no one else. Well, aside from everything being absolute, there's absolutely no comparison in this world. I'm watching the absolutes dancing. And the voids. Concepts. Allegories. Metaphors. Spiked heels. Absent ladies. And present public. What a bunch of absolutes, I whisper, helpless. I whisper in the ear of one of the guests. My brows are knit. I'm frowning again. And someone interrupts with an inopportune sneeze. How dare he. Show-off. The absolute lord of concepts. Pure abstractions. Cigarette. Dust. Smoke. Petrified guest. And phantoms. A squirrel keeps going by. And keeps dancing. A dancing mouse. Music at every interval around my soul. Or every absolute reduced at once to utter nothingness.

I have to describe what's happening to me. And I have to describe it in the same way. I have to study it. I have to make it mine. There are many things that are. The seasons of the year are. There they are. Just like we are out there. Hatred and envy are also out there. They are an integral part of every man. They take root in every inch of the heart. In every piece of flesh. In every man. In every body. I'm a body I don't understand. What am I? I ask. And I laugh. I don't know. Yet I do. Because I have never said what I am, though I often ask myself. I will be, I always say. And time passes, and I see the seasons. They are. Yes, they are. And then I bow my head and sink in sunsets. No, it isn't a child's wheel. It's neither birth. Nor death. I won't define it. I'd rather destroy it. Or let them destroy me. It was time for us to sink in the abyss. Silence. Nothing is there. Nothing exists. Except multitudes of broken things. There is nothing after silence.

To see the distance then. To see it standing, and to see it made into a body. With breath. With eyes. With deaths. Then to see absences. Memories. To see films. Again. Without enthusiasm. Without beauty. To see it standing and sitting, writing poetry. And to see the waves of the sea. And to see the sun. Or the moon. Or to discover that they are always born. And they always die. As always. And they always sleep. They spend summers away leaving winters behind. They're drawn to autumns. Sundays. And birthdays. They go to discos. And get tired of dancing. And they talk. How many people have I slept with? How many men do I get up with? And the next morning, the morning, the mirror that grows each day until it turns into a ball of fire. I'd give up everything I own to escape this damned world. I'd sell my eyes and my legs. I'd sell my ways. And my sorrows. I'd become a sailor and sail. To see the distance then. We returned by foot that same day on the rails of life. Through tunnels of death. To see springs then. And sadnesses. And I'm not dissatisfied. I keep my distance. So I'm not taken by surprise. So that life surprises me.

What radiant colors. What childhoods. What wombs or mornings. White walls all around the length and width and depth of my soul. The piano surrounded by men or women and children. The piano plays. I was listening to it, off to the side. Pale. Way down inside me. Way beyond the sounds. Throughout the sunset, said the rosary of a dawn. Because dawns have rosaries. And also nightingales. Absurd. As absurd as sunset. They start cooking breakfast. They start dressing at the break of day. They become as absurd as the sun. Or morning. But the piano, so absurd. As absurd as day. As night itself. Like the piano. They start playing. They start singing. They start reciting. They start lecturing. As absurd as noon. Who can understand them? Absurd. Who can figure them out? Absurd. From each sun. From each new sunshine. Only the rosary of dawn remains. And the radiance of morning. Absurd. Cast off the sheets. Open the bed. Absurd. Casting through the window. Absurd. Casting. What colors. What childhoods. What dawns. Absurd.

Watching everything, said the spectator. *Profane Comedy.* The party. Or time, said the director. And fate, said the boy. And my baby teeth, he added, pointing to the void. And fate, repeated the boy. And this time he pointed to the pianist. Music always starts suddenly, said the pianist suddenly. And he surprised them. Children always crawl showing their baby teeth. Flies are always killed suddenly. And he surprised them again. Suddenly fate escaped. Suddenly the pianist. And the painter. Suddenly the spectator. Where there is no distance between the spectacle and the performance. Only the fate that marches. Silence, silence, please. This is when the hostess comes in, sits down, and surprises them again. The guests looked at each other surprised, and surprised each other again. Suddenly the piano played one of the keys of the pianist. How strange! And it surprised them again.

Hear this. Bastards. Don't think that anybody or anything is going to kill me. Not the vinaigrette olives. Not the coffee cake of the most bitter expectation. When after all, it's too late. What is hunger? The hunger that devours me. Hunger. No, no, I'll tell the olives. No, no, I'll tell the salad dressings. No, no, to the vegetables. No, no, to the green giants. No, no, to the liquor of dreams. And to the coffee cake of feeling good. And to the stuffed stomach. I know the story quite well. I know what it's all about. I know all its arguments by heart. I swear No! for all the gold in the world, No! and No! No! No! No! I can't stay seated and end up feeling full or bloated when the same crap as always repeats itself. And appetizers and desserts turn my stomach. Nauseated, I bid farewell. Nauseated. And I do not resign. Nor do I give up. No! and no! and no!

Now I laugh at everything and not for the irony. Even though my eyes are closing. And I'm not asleep. How many more minutes do I have left? Is it true that they'll shoot me soon? And why not now? I'm not afraid of guns. Let them pull the trigger. Let them kill me. I told you they could pull the trigger. Why don't they just pull the trigger and finish me off? Answer me. Why don't they just pull it? We're not immortals, and a shot in the temple would end it all. What's stopping them from pulling it? Why is it so hard now that I'm so far away from my base and it would be so easy to pull that trigger? What's the big deal? Why don't they just finish pulling it? Why? Unless it's too hard to point at me with a pistol. And become murderers. But they're already that. Is it their guilty conscience. You know, the little worm. And nothing else. No shit. Cowardice. And nothing else. Cowardice. And all the rest. Pantomimes!

The sunset is purple. Then I discover night. Beside the night, half an orange open. Slices. The sky is starry at the party. And there is an orange fire. The bell rings. Orange behind orange. Here in the living room. Here in the courtyard. The teacher spoke. The spectator spoke. The producer spoke. We saw the film. We saw the ambulance. We saw the teacher swallow the purple sunset. And his nostalgia was yellow. Canaries are yellow. And form is yellow. And hope is yellow. But what do I care? Ha! Ha! Ha! Ha! And I took my partner out to dance. I see everything. Everything. Everything. I see clearly. There's absolutely no confusion. Everything is transparent. He swallows another draught of sleep. I remember. And I drink. But I see it very clearly. So clear. I faint. I fall. And die. Heh! Heh! Heh! Heh! I die. And I don't move. I die. Heh! I move. Ha! I die.

A scene. A fate. A crawl. A mitt. I blow on the candles. And cut a piece of cake. I blow on another candle. And eat my cake. I see my mother sitting all along the family grounds. I see billowing flags of love moving up and down all along the national grounds. And in a hidden corner a night shadow smells fishy. Smells burnt. Something was burning. The mother asks: What burned? The boy shows his baby teeth. The boy's mitt, catching butterflies, comes and goes along the family grounds. I blow out the candles once and for all. To see if everything ends. The world's birthday. The frisky ol' goat turned sixty. This took place in a park. In a forest with big trees. With roots. With bridges. With brushes. With deaths. In a forest. Seated. A birthday was painted. Two birthdays. Three birthdays of green seasons. Green. Green.

Sunsets repeat themselves throughout my life. Railroad tracks come and go, decrepit with years. Throughout my years. A tree falls. A war breaks out. A lion dies. And I roar, roar. Or creak, creak. Throughout my life. Many violent deaths. Many happy years. Along the streetcar. Looking over its length. And its width. Long or short. Short circuit. I cut it all along. Cut. Shorter. Shorter. Longer. Longer. The movie film. Reduced. Increased. To nothing. To utter nothingness. In shadow, in dust, in nothing. Nothing.

Repeat yourself, universe. See if you dare to repeat yourself once and for all. Spring shouted beside itself. And turned into summer. See if you dare to kill winter. And summer repeated itself. See if you dare to stay young once and for all. And youth repeated itself for generations and generations and generations of green seasons. Green. Green. Am I still green? Where is spring? What's this tale about? What's this story of green seasons about? Green. Green.

What's it all about? Ha, ha, ha, ha! Spring laughed. And gave a bud. Fall laughed. And plucked a flower. Winter laughed. And snow fell. Summer laughed. And I fainted from the heat. What's it all about? Ha, ha, ha, ha! What's your death about? Look at me. And stop asking questions. Shout: I don't understand it. And rot. Or die. Or paint, said the painter turned into a forest of bitterness that was still painted green. Green. Green. And bitter. Bitterness. What's it all about? Heh, heh, heh, heh! And envy laughed. I'm happy. Happy. Happy. And just then it set off an orgy of capital sins ending with these lines by Rimbaud:

—Oh! tous les vices, colère, luxure:

—magnifique, la luxure…

A tree is still a wonder. And I'm amazed that it is—said the architect entangled in pure reflection. The first floor is the one that leans farthest out the window of life. The chimney is like dust, smoke, wind. He goes on and on and on thinking about the chimney. He smokes a cigarette. He lights it. How strange. I'm lighting it. There's only one power here. It's the power of wind. It's the power of water. It's the power of generations. Of grandparents. And of great-grandchildren. And of my ball of the world turning another year older. And of the song to nothingness. You show me your teeth. They're baby teeth. And I create a world for you. Like ostriches. A dream of a night reeking of sulfur. And a new season is created, a fifth season. That knows nothing. That ignores everything. That passes everything. Like life itself. It is created. Over the four seasons. A new season. Or the song of nothingness.

It is a cry I hear. A hidden clamor. Like that of a beast. Like that of a camel that became a lion. It is my birth. I am the boy. I am the clamor of silence. I am its pallor. And its hidden tremble. Death filled this puddle with such a scream. Leave me alone—cried the boy. And he played dead. This has been a dead cry. A cry that seems dead. It seems that death turn into deaths. They are born. Born. They grow. Grow. They seem. Leave me alone—he cried. And still seemed. I repeat. Seemed. Only seemed. And piano. Piano. Pianissimo. Always. Always. Always. And forever. He seems to be alive. He looks like death. It seems that death always remains. As if it were alive. But it is dead.

Let's say that sometimes things are different. But they are. And it's better to do it right the first time. Than to have to go back and fix it. Proverbs are too. Or traffic signs. Stop. And the same boots of destiny still are. And the same butterflies. The boy laughs as always. Showing his seven baby teeth as always.

Life pains me—said the philosopher. Newspapers pain me. Days behind nights behind days. Seas behind seas behind tides pain me. Buildings behind parks behind doves pain me. Businessmen behind money behind usury pain me. Waves behind histories behind people pain me. Behind skeletons behind shadows. Behind phantoms of shadows. Behind eyes. Behind falling tears. *"Flow without sorrow, tears, falling."*

Another flash of chaos or death, said anonymous. All is semblance. All is shadow. All is stone. Or dream. Or nothing. I have seen the boots of destiny rising. I have seen the shit of destiny rising. I have seen the bootblacks of destiny rising. Rising over the same boots of death. What is this? What is still creeping and crawling? Shoes tremble. Or boots. Tremble. And build fires. Matches of fire. And I keep repeating myself. I, the unknown, the mute, the invisible. I can't understand anything. I don't want to understand anything. There's nothing to understand.

I don't understand it. I don't understand it. I don't understand it, noted the spokesman. It's three, it's four, it's five. And suddenly three, four, and five disappear. And the sixth character appears. A telegram appears, or a letter. The father appears. And grandparents appear. And great-grandparents and great-grandchildren. And baby teeth keep chasing me. Or suddenly, yes, suddenly, I miss the butterfly. And I can't find it. The butterfly has died. And the boy laughs. I don't understand it. I don't understand it. I don't understand it. And everyone thought. Could it be the butterfly. Could it be fate. Could it be the architect. Could it be the mother. Could it be the hostess. Could it be life. And so be it, they said. And they repeated: amen. For the rest of time. And they started creating, building, dreaming, drinking, laughing. Also for the rest of time. And inventing episodes, dramas, sorrows, scenes, and nostalgias. They started looking in ecstasy at the infinite. And pointed out four seasons of the year. Yes, they pointed out spring, summer, autumn, winter. And surprised at themselves again they showed their baby teeth. Some were drinking milk. And cognac—others. And whiskey—others. And others said: amen. And so be it for the rest of time.

That's the way it goes. Just think, I was a powerful man. Now I'm a bootblack. Just think, I've also got a baby tooth. It's the only one I've got left. I've been turning with the wheel of fortune over the roads of the world for more than sixty years. And now my boots, ah, my boots are too tight. They don't fit me right. And soon, either the mitt or the teeth of destiny will say once more: I don't understand. Or feel it. But that's the way it goes. First, a child. Later spring. Or fall. The prince kisses Sleeping Beauty. I wake up startled and stunned. And I see how leaves fall. And we're back in winter or summer again. That's just the way it goes. And the three or four of us will disappear. And the tenth or the seventh will come. And click. Clack. That's the way the wheel of fortune turns. A powerful man. And a bootblack. That's the way it goes.

I don't mean to philosophize or preach—said the teacher. But would you believe that I can still dance. And I like to dance. I have died many times. But I bounce back. Just like a ball. And I dance. I die. Or I believe that I'm dead. Then I discover that death is only a new movement. A new birth. A sacred yes. And I show my baby teeth. That's why I'm the teacher. Just think, it all boils down to nothing. But there are things I just don't understand, and I'll never be able to understand them. I don't want to understand them. I place my hand on my head. I don't care to understand them. I'd rather own them. Put on my boots. Wear them until their soles tear. Until they're ruined. I'm a bootblack. But I don't clean my own boots. I get them muddy and wear them out. Which confuses the big shots, now even more than before. They still can't figure it out. How they shine. How my boots gleam whether they're dirty or clean. How they're mended. How they sparkle and gleam. Without looking clean. Without the bootblack cleaning them. And now I understand it all. I see it all so clear. Clear. And they started dancing. Hostesses. Teachers. Bootblacks. Architects. I don't understand it. It's clear. The sky is so bright. The star. The boot. The bootblack. I understand it all. I don't understand it. I don't understand it. I don't understand it. Yet I understand it. All. All. All.

III. The Intimate Diary of Solitude

1. Death of Poetry

Withdrawn into the peace of this desert,
Along with some books, few but wise,
I live in conversation with the deceased,
And listen to the dead with my eyes.

—Quevedo, *From the Tower*

The Adventures of Mariquita Samper

I was trudging along after filming part of *Profane Comedy*—said the Narrator—when suddenly I saw *The Intimate Diary of Solitude* was already playing at the Arts Cinema. I bought my ticket. The usher handed me the stub. I bought some popcorn and sat down to watch *The Adventures of Mariquita Samper.* I looked around the Arts Cinema. It was spacious and comfortable with four escape doors: Exit One. Exit Two. Exit Three. Exit Four. Though each door walked a character from *The Intimate Diary of Solitude.* A total of four characters took up the front row. And although there were only four, or five, or six characters, they multiplied, doubling and tripling as the scenes progressed. I ate a piece of popcorn. Fell fast asleep. And didn't wake up until the lights came on. And then I immediately began to write the first scene of *The Intimate Diary of Solitude,* entitled *The Adventures of Mariquita Samper.*

Epigraph: "A closed mouth catches no flies."

My name is Mariquita Samper. I work at Macy's. My job is to make up people who don't like to make themselves up. I'm an artist. I'm the makeup artist of the characters of this fiction that separates fantasy from reality. And I'm shocked by the things that happen. A lady asked me to paint her dog's nails.

Lady, I said, I'm Mariquita Samper, Macy's makeup artist. Not a canine pedicurist. Wuff! Wuff!—barked the dog. And I was so sorry. Then a guy with a perfume tray passed by, and a perfume that reeked like "a barking doesn't bite" pervaded the store. I caught a whiff of sirens. Saw toys tooting. And a whole pack of police dogs came charging at us. Yes, it's Macy's, the World's Largest Store! Yes, it's New York. I ran for my life as soon as I heard the threatening sound of the pack of police dogs. Perfume and makeup went up in flames. Not so reality and fantasy. I took a cab to Caffé degli Artisti. And headed straight for the ladies' room. Took off my high heels and false lashes. Wiped off some makeup. Left some rouge on. Dried my lips. And ordered a campari and soda. That's when my friend, the French professor, arrived. I was a bundle of nerves. I kept gazing into his eyes. A professor and a Macy's makeup artist. I forgot to mention that my name is Giannina Braschi. And that I agreed to play Mariquita—said Giannina Braschi—for commercial gain. And she flashed Mariquita's gold tooth as she laughed. I've written books while making women up. I write on their faces. I illuminate their shadows and discover their craters and even their volcanoes that suddenly erupt. I write wrinkles on the faces of October and on the memories of November. Oh, Uri, Uri—for that was the French professor's name. Uriberto Eisensweig speaks with a French accent. It's not really an accent. It's a speech impediment called *sticky tongue*. Uriberto pronounces his r's like h's. His little catch is like Mariquita's red freckles. Like her red-dyed hair. Like her gold tooth. Uriberto is bearded and hairy like a monkey. I write these black pages on his black beard. I smiled at him. He smiled at me. And we left the café with the campari and soda in hand, as Bengal lights glared all over the menu and the makeup of the open book that is being written. Uri showed me a line. An oblique line at the back of the café. And it suddenly turned into the Narrator who was sitting to our left. No, please, not this nightmare, not again. If I haven't arranged the date in *The Intimate Diary of Solitude*. If Uri is not yet Uri, and Giannina is not yet Giannina. Suddenly everything fades. Everything escapes. Everything turns to solitude. Solitude is a well full of water. Here in this well—as I open my front door. Oh, Uri, Uri. Longing for Uri. A void. Enormous. Smooth. Smooth. Like a piece of clothing. In a building where clothing is bought and makeup is sold, a TV screen appears. The Narrator is screening Mariquita Samper. Suddenly there is no way to measure the distance between the Narrator screening Mariquita on TV and me climbing the stairs to my apartment. The doorman opens the car door. Mariquita steps out of the car. The doorman carries her packages. Mariquita smiles suggestively. Lifts her skirt a bit. And leans toward the TV. The Narrator tries to penetrate the intimacy of her heart. But there are so many doors that open and close. There are so many TV sets that turn on and off. And there is a white dove that escapes from Mariquita Samper's heart and turns into a handkerchief when she stares at it. Her eyes glaze over as she follows the flying handkerchief. She opens her purse. Looks for something inside. Can't remember what it was she was looking for. On her way to the station, looking for a nickel, she finds her train ticket. On the train that takes her around the circumference of her solitude, she stares at a landscape of water. She looks out the window that delimits the borders of her solitude and sees the handkerchief's wings waving: goodbye-goodbye. Then Mariquita looks away from the window and looks at the open pages of

The Intimate Diary of Solitude. I really like this phrase—she says. And she underlines it as I underline the same phrase that Mariquita Samper underlined while reading the adventures of her own solitude. She opens her purse, takes out a compact, and powders her face. She dabs some rouge on her cheeks and paints her lips. It's been exactly one hour since she repeated everything that she read in the book. The train pulls into that station where I can still distinguish the day she fell in love with me from the day I left her. But it's already midnight, and I'm still watching *The Adventures of Mariquita Samper* on TV. Suddenly, I'm back in the theater buying popcorn. Suddenly, the white dove flies out of the TV movie screen and sits on my hands. Suddenly, the dove widens the distance again, and Mariquita is back on the screen feeding the dove my popcorn. Mariquita gets off the train. Runs to 6th Avenue and 34th Street. Goes up to her apartment. Looks for another nickel. Takes the elevator. Goes down to the street to mail a letter to the Narrator. Takes the subway to 3rd Avenue on page 15 and stops to think in the heat of her solitude. She powders her forehead again, and her face glows like a ball of fire. She hears the sirens of fire trucks drowning out the sound of a transistor radio. The Narrator turns up the volume of *The Adventures of Mariquita Samper.* He feels his hand picking up speed with every word he writes. And the rhythm of life and writing accelerates. The car driving Mariquita down the highway can hardly stop like the Narrator writing this diary. The world is a great grammatical system. Mariquita re-underlines this phrase that reminds her of the white dove flying away. Goodbye-goodbye—she repeats. And some red Bengal lights interrupt the rhythm of her blood. She opens her purse, and there at the bottom is a phrase she forgot to underline. This crossword puzzle of things blinds me and erases distance. Then the Narrator wrote that Mariquita was about to go to bed. And as soon as he wrote it, Mariquita began to nod off. And she took a cab home. The doorman took her packages. Mariquita went up to her apartment. The Narrator turned off the radio, and Mariquita's image slowly faded from the TV screen. But the Narrator left Mariquita's picture on the screen of his solitude. He thought that his script should be written in her diary. And that the diary was slowly repeating what was already part of the solitude of Mariquita's heart. He turned off the light. And she went to sleep in order to maintain the distance that she covered between the contents of her dreams and the intimacy of her solitude. But, before going to bed, he set the alarm clock of life to awaken Mariquita's solitude from a deep sleep. He rested his head on her diary's pillow of solitude. He got up an hour later, half-asleep, and watched *The Adventures of Mariquita Samper* again. I am not through yet. Don't limit my existence—Mariquita told the Narrator. She got out of bed and began to sing. All I need is love. Love. Love. And she drifted back to sleep. She got up an hour later and sang it again. And quit her solitude for good. She read the intimate diary of her solitude again. All I need is love. Love. Love. And she continued arguing with the printed words of *The Intimate Diary of Solitude.* A party. A disco—she said. And on saying, "All I need is love," she started dancing, flooding the words with music and joy. The blaring disco that Mariquita had just discovered in her heart woke up the Narrator. Mariquita yelled to him, "All I need is love. Love. Love." And she continued correcting every page of *The Intimate Diary of Solitude.* She drew a heart on one of them. And a star on another. She laughed at the distance that her hand crossed at the bottom of her coat pocket. She revved up her diary's roaring engine. She laughed at the TV screen where the Narrator had tried to limit her existence to a parenthesis between one phrase and another. In addition, she had erased the line that she had underlined and replaced it with: All I need is love. Love. Love. When the Narrator reviewed the pages of his diary, he found that Mariquita had limited his existence. And had replaced him with a revolution of mad rhythms. Rhythms of love. Love—Mariquita called it. Love. She had let her hair down. She had smeared black ink all over her diary. She had, at length, fallen in love. Or in the words of solitude, she had written the first fragment of *The Intimate Diary of Solitude.*

Life and Works of Berta Singerman

Backstage all the characters of *The Intimate Diary of Solitude* are getting dressed. The TV is on, and Mariquita Samper is dressed up as Berta Singerman. New York. New York. It's the year 2000, when Berta Singerman forfeited her American citizenship and went to live in Moscow out of love for Uriberto Eisensweig. In this show, Uriberto Eisensweig is exactly 30 years old, 20 years younger than Berta Singerman, which makes this the toughest role that Mariquita has ever played in her entire life. Mariquita had to gain 30 pounds and age considerably. She had to draw crow's feet around her eyes. In reality, Mariquita is 30 years old, the same age as Uriberto. In reality, Uriberto and Mariquita have been in love all of their lives. Judging from the looks of both protagonists, they're in the prime of their lives. One is Capricorn and the other, Aquarius. December 30th and February 5th. A fortune-teller had already predicted it: "You'll marry five times without having married at all"—she told Mariquita in New York. "You'll forfeit your American citizenship. You'll fall in love five times with the same man, and you'll think five times that he is a different man. You'll understand that the same man also fell in love with five different women who were the same woman. But while making love the fifth time with the same man who was a different man, you'll reach the peak of your artistic career. And the fame of your myth and your story will make you shine as the greatest artist produced in the brief history of humanity." We are in the year 2000, when Berta Singerman turned 50. My name is really Mariquita Samper, and I'm from Puerto Rico. I live in New York City. My name is really Uriberto Singerman, and I'm playing the role of Uriberto Eisensweig. Mariquita also goes by the name of Berta Eisensweig, usurping my name, or taking Mariquita Singerman's or Berta Samper's. Name games are all the same. After all, every name is a usurpation of a fragment of my life and works. Every name is a different name in another history of humanity. I was just telling Uriberto Eisensweig that it's not easy being Mariquita Singerman and playing Berta Samper because it's not easy being in two different versions of *The Intimate Diary of Solitude*. In spite of what the writer of this diary thinks, I am very far away from Uriberto Eisensweig and New York City. In spite of what might be or is, I'm simultaneously in New York and Moscow. It's exactly midnight on a winter night in New York. Here I am in perfect sync with the time and date of New York and Moscow. And here I am, in the year 1985, recording these pages of history. How many lies are told in the name of art and literature! I was born in San Juan, Puerto Rico. I grew up near the waves of the sea. They showed me that lies are true. And that I should come and go as I please. Like ships or waves, I'm constantly moving from place to place. I don't know how to stay still for a single instant. I'm an unbalanced woman by nature. And like the waves of the sea, I'm always resisting attacks and insults. I'm vulnerable in love affairs. I'm always, or almost always, something different, and I'll never figure it out. Today for instance, I got a Christmas present. I opened it and there was a snowball inside. Sometimes I cry just to cry, and sometimes I laugh just to laugh. I'm fickle with my affections. I rejected the sea a thousand times. I repeat that I left Puerto Rico at 18 never to return. I crossed all of Europe in two years. I returned to the sea and wound up in Manhattan. I've lived longer here than anywhere else. I'm an artisan of life by nature. Now I understand what I used to understand a long time ago, although I'm not sure I remember what it was. I'll never forget what I remembered as a child, and I entered its secret secretly. Now that I have this snowball, I ask myself if life is a snowball. I was 23 exactly 23 years ago. The truth is, I landed in Moscow yesterday, and today I'm 50 years old. Wasn't that what the Narrator wanted me to say? I'm sorry, but I'm only 30 even though you make me look like I'm 50. I doubt that the readers are as stupid as you. I'm also sorry that I believed that I fell in love with Uriberto. You wanted me to fall in love with him. Didn't you, Narrator? Too bad Uriberto doesn't exist. I'm sorry to deceive you, reader. On the other hand, I'm also Uriberto Eisensweig. I'm sorry to be simultaneously what I write. The Narrator is also a product of my imagination. What I write seems unreal, but it's true. I want to lie, but I don't. And sometimes I cry just to cry. I am a man who has had many loves in his life—said Uriberto Samper. But he immediately corrects himself and says, "Sadly, a single love so confused is more than enough. Don't you think so, Mariquita?" As soon as I came to New York, I fell in love with a book. After I wrote *Assault on Time*, I immediately wrote *Profane Comedy*. I left for Puerto Rico. Returned to Europe. Changed my name more than twenty times. And grew rich with lies. I pretended you were Uriberto and I was Mariquita.

I walked around New York City dreaming of making that great trip to Moscow. I renounced my American citizenship. I landed in Moscow. I gave more than 100 poetry readings. I read "This is the Child Mother of the circus." I read "Eggs are months and days too." I acquired the wisdom of *Poems of the World*. I became a fortune-teller, a magician, and then, Shepherd Giannina. I defended memory. I preached of poetic eggs. Everyone thought I was mad, and the masses adored me. I turned poetry into a circus of lies. I've lied all my life. I'm a liar by vocation and history. I made up this story as I was walking alone in New York one day. It was easy. I burst out laughing at life. I'm such an idiot! And I started to cry. In reality, I'm 30. In reality, Uriberto is Uriberto and I'm Berta Singerman. In reality, he is 30 and I'm 50. In reality, we haven't seen each other in five years. I met Uriberto on a street in New York this year. The truth is that I haven't spoken with him and he hasn't spoken with me in five years. In reality, it was the Narrator who insisted that I tell the truth. But the truth is: I always lie. I'm so much happier since I broke up with Uriberto. I'm glad you left me. Sometimes I'd like to see you. I'm not always happy you left. Sometimes I still write about Uriberto and Mariquita when I should be writing about Uriberto and Berta. It's not easy to tell the truth when you're writing lies. But this is just another angle of the diary narrating my solitude. Uriberto is alone. So is Mariquita. Berta is the only one who dreams of companionship. Berta fell in love with the same man five times. She changed his personality. She made each man live in a different place. They all believed Berta was the woman of their lives. They all believed Berta Singerman's lies. But Berta didn't know how to love anyone but herself. Berta was another lie. But sometimes I dream of living her life. Berta died the day she discovered that all of this was a way of telling solitude that she was still accompanied, when in truth, she was alone writing another lie in *The Intimate Diary of Solitude.*

The Things That Happen to Men in New York!

The things that happen to men in New York! This is written as an exclamation. It is, of course, an exaggeration—says the Narrator. These things don't only happen in New York. They happen in Havana and Berlin. They happen in Madrid and Moscow. And they don't only happen to men. They happen to women too. I thought it was strange that I couldn't find the men's room—said Mariquita Samper. I asked where the ladies' room was—said Uriberto Eisensweig, dressed up as Berta Singerman. After I left the restroom—said the Narrator—I sat down to watch *The Things That Happen to Men in New York*. Maybe this is why I'm always changing my name. I don't like being called Mariquita Samper when I'm really playing Berta Singerman, and I'm a lesbian. Mariquita, the fairy drag queen! Backstage, Mariquita Samper dresses up as Uriberto Eisensweig. And Uriberto Eisensweig dresses up as Berta Samper. Don't you know that I'm Uriberto Singerman? And that Uriberto Samper is none other than Berta Eisensweig? Listen, sir, to the things that happen to men in New York! Mariquita: "It is I, Uriberto Eisensweig!" Suddenly, the curtain falls. Apparently, the public likes *The Things That Happen to Men in New York*—says the Narrator. Why else would they applaud so much? Deep down, they're asking for an encore. Uriberto gets a bigger hand when he plays Mariquita Samper.

Bravo! Bravo! Encore! Listen, lady, to the things that happen to women in New York! They think that they're women, but they're men. They think that they're men, but they're women. Backstage is Mariquita Samper's mother. I don't want you dressing up as Uriberto. What thrill do you get from scandalizing people? Mama, don't you see them laughing? Don't you see them having fun? Deep down in every man there is a woman. Deep down in every woman there is a man. Things are men and women. Apples look for pears. And pears love peaches. Listen, sir, to the things that happen to pears in New York! Nothing new. We already knew that men like pears. And that peaches like oranges. We also knew that an orange is an orange. And that an apple is a peach. I didn't know that—says the apple's mother. I thought my daughter liked peaches. But pears? Gentlemen, ladies—she says, placing her hand on her head. I didn't know that happened to women in New York. Ladies, gentlemen—says the pear's father solemnly—I didn't know that it would happen to my son. But the things that happen to men and women!—sing the pear and the peach. The apple and the orange join in the chorus:

> Oh, the things that happen to men in New York! Oh, the things that happen to women in New York! Bravo! Bravo! THE END of this scene.
> And THE END of another daily episode that I live in New York.
> Signed: The Narrator

Everyone says that truths are lies. Everyone says that lies are true. But I'm the only one who knows that I'm alone writing another cheap illusion. And with a tear in my eye, with a tear that gives me away, I laugh at the irony—writing *The Intimate Diary of Solitude* really takes its toll on me.

The Queen of Beauty, Charm, and Coquetry

Her name was Anna Mayo. It took her a while to figure out how to become a part of *The Intimate Diary of Solitude*. But she seized the perfect opportunity. An ad appeared in *The Intimate Diary of Solitude*'s newspaper. WANTED: journalist to write a column on the Queen of Beauty, Charm, and Coquetry. Anna Mayo immediately called Uriberto Eisensweig and told him that she'd apply for the position. Uriberto Eisensweig owned the newspaper and wanted his favorite girlfriend, Mariquita, to be crowned the Queen of Beauty, Charm, and Coquetry. I admit it's true, but I wouldn't put it in writing—says Uriberto. It must be painstakingly planned so that no one knows that she is our pick. Mariquita Samper had to lose 20 pounds. She developed a sweet tooth after having played Berta Singerman. The newspaper and magazine photos, as well as Anna Mayo's chronicles detailing her incredible beauty and extraordinary grace, all pointed out that Mariquita was a bit chubby. To improve her looks, she dyed her hair red and had fake freckles surgically implanted on her cheeks. Mariquita definitely looks like a charm queen with that red hair and those wonderful freckles—wrote Anna Mayo over and over again. Burning the candle at both ends, Anna Mayo spent day and night publicizing Mariquita's beauty, and day and night Mariquita radiated coquetry. She laughed all day and all night long.

Men stopped to stare. But she kept her distance. In order to become the Queen of Beauty, Charm, and Coquetry, she had to be alone. That's what the reign of beauty's solitude was all about. It wasn't hard to seduce the readers of *The Intimate Diary of Solitude*. Anna Mayo and Uriberto took care of that. Reviews appeared on Mariquita's remarkable versatility. You have to overlook her little defects. After all, she can afford the few extra pounds. Besides, you can't blame Mariquita's beauty for the weight of Berta's solitude. Suddenly, everyone bowed to her in reverence. She was proclaimed—Her Majesty, the Queen. Anna Mayo was also proclaimed—Journalist of the Year. *The Intimate Diary of Solitude* was the most widely read newspaper. And Uriberto, in his role as the owner, made millions. They met at the Narrator's house to celebrate their triumph. It was sensational. Overnight, Berta Singerman and Uriberto Samper's beauty and popularity flourished. But an enormous burden of solitude followed their fame. They were worried. They were accomplices. Backstage they reconsidered everything. They bounced it around. They didn't like it. It looked too much like reality. There is no queen in this story. Mariquita stepped down from her throne. Uriberto confessed he wasn't in love with her. Anna lost her job at the newspaper. Something is missing here—said the Narrator. You don't know how to pretend. What's wrong with Mariquita being proclaimed the Queen of Beauty, Charm, and Coquetry? Nothing's wrong, Narrator, but I don't want to be the Queen of Solitude. The Narrator dropped the curtain on this episode, stamped it *cancelled*, and scribbled out this fragment of *The Intimate Diary of Solitude* in black ink.

Gossip

It was all a fraud—declared other newspapers, as they slung the mud at Mariquita and Uriberto. Everybody knows how rumors get around. You don't have to search the world over to know that it's all cheap talk, but it really takes its toll—said Anna Mayo in one of her chronicles. Mariquita had to pay a steep price to become a beauty queen. Let's not talk about Berta Singerman's forfeiting her American citizenship. Not to mention the truth about *The Things That Happen to Men in New York*! What a scandal it was to find out that Uriberto was Mariquita! Even poor Berta Singerman, who had loved him so much, though that she gave him too much love and too much passion only for him to become Mariquita. True, Mariquita won the prize for beauty, charm, and coquetry. But it cost her a fortune. She had to pay in freckles, and now she can't dye her hair black. That was just another piece of gossip that rained on Mariquita's glory. Even now, a while later, people still talk of Uriberto and Berta's daughter. They wonder if she is anything like Mariquita Samper. That's another story in *The Intimate Diary of Solitude*. That's another theatrical scene. Now they're saying that Mariquita is the love child of Uriberto and Berta's scandalous affair. She had to lose her innocence. She dresses like a goody-goody. She dresses like a sweet-sixteen. But a playboy seduces her. And Mariquita, lily of the valley, has lost her virginity—again! It was Uriberto,

Uriberto the playboy—wrote Anna Mayo in one of her gossip columns. In no time, gossip was rolling like a snowball. Uriberto first took Berta as his lover, and then he took his own daughter, who is also named Mariquita Samper! But I thought Uriberto was Mariquita. But it turns out Uriberto is Mariquita's father and that Mariquita is not Mariquita. It's just another piece of gossip running around New York. Even history repeats itself. Berta had a daughter named Mariquita. And Mariquita had a son named Uriberto, who was a professor before he became Mariquita. Then Mariquita became Berta Singerman. Then she forfeited her American citizenship and went to live in Russia. Then two Mariquitas and two Uribertos fell in love. There were generations and generations of gossip. Other fragments of *The Intimate Diary of Solitude* were written. Other articles were written too. But gossip became fantasy. But gossip became reality. The gossip about Uriberto and Mariquita bore Mariquita Singerman and Mariquita Eisensweig. As well as Uriberto Samper and Uriberto Singerman. The race of gossip reproduced, and Anna Mayo was born. Generations of gossip reproduced, and solitude was born. I used to think that gossip made up the race of solitude—wrote the Narrator in Anna Mayo's intimate diary. I also thought that Mariquita's solitude is just gossip. Even Uriberto's solitude is gossip. And so is Anna Mayo. The newspaper, *The Intimate Diary of Solitude,* is gossip too. After all, it went bankrupt because Anna Mayo ran out of gossip to tell. Even though my gossiping hand writes alone, I'll never run out of solitude's gossip, even if I'm stripped of meaning. I mean life. Ha! Ha! Ha! Ha!

Portrait of Giannina Braschi

Dear Narrator:

I've got a really big problem. No one takes me seriously. They all love Mariquita, and when I tell them that I'm Mariquita, they just laugh. Everyone thinks that I made up the race of beauty, charm, and coquetry just because I made up the race of gossip and the race of solitude. No one wants to see *Portrait of Giannina Braschi*. My friends call me up and say, "Mariquita, Mariquita, what's the gossip of the day? What's going on in *The Intimate Diary of Solitude* today?" But they don't know that I am an autobiography. They don't know that I am *Portrait of Giannina Braschi*. My friends have told me I owe my existence to their gossip and their lives. And they're right. I'm only called Giannina when Mariquita dresses up as Berta Singerman. I'm only called Giannina when Mariquita falls in love with Uriberto—Berta Singerman once said through Mariquita Samper's mouth. You know something—and I say this only to the reader—these friends of mine do exist—although I'd never tell them that. They're not figments of my imagination. I see them every day, or at least once a week when we get together at Mariquita's to laugh at *The Intimate Diary of Solitude*. My friends are Uriberto, Mariquita, Berta, the Narrator, the race of gossip, and *The Intimate Diary of Solitude*. Little by little, you'll meet my other friends who widen the circle of my solitude even more—said the Narrator. You already know Anna Mayo, the journalist famous for writing the race of gossip and the race of the Mariquitas and the Uribertos. But you still haven't met Honorata Pagan, the fortune-teller who predicted that Berta Singerman would forfeit her Russian citizenship. This fortune-teller, named Honorata Pagan, was also the one who told me I had no right to complain if they confused me with Mariquita. "Giannina, you're a celebrity. But your friends believe more in your lies than in your autobiography. You chose to be the author of this work. You chose your profession. So it's your own fault if they don't take you seriously. And so what if your friends love Mariquita more than you? Frankly, you already know that she is more beautiful, more charming, and more coquettish. She has a new love to talk about every day. And what do you have? Just a pen and paper to write your *Intimate Diary of Solitude*." Honorata Pagan's fame skyrocketed even before her predictions came through. Whenever I went, she went with me. Uriberto consulted her on some of his love affairs. Honorata had told him, "Uriberto, you will deflower Berta Singerman's daughter—your own daughter, Mariquita. You will be an incestuous father." What Honorata never got to tell him is that it would happen on stage. What she never got to tell him was that her prophecies were also fiction. Enough of your lies, Mariquita. I'm going to do Giannina's portrait. I'm going to turn Mariquita into Giannina Samper. But don't whine and complain when you're the punch-line, Giannina. Don't complain when you're Mariquita, Giannina. That's when the portrait of my intimate solitude became part of the diary. The painter was Vita Giorgi. I met Vita at a Soho gallery where Berta was giving Uriberto a show. On exhibit there were all of the portraits of Mariquita from the time she lost her virginity at 15 until the time she became the first Puerto Rican to forfeit her American citizenship and live in Moscow. And a new character was introduced there. An impudent, devilish clown by the name of Giannina Braschi—said the Narrator. With a furrowed brow and a hoarse throat, she burst out laughing like thunder or a steep cliff, and Mariquita Samper leaped out of the *Portrait of Giannina*. Even though I was by myself, I imagined that Mariquita and Uriberto, Berta Singerman, Honorata Pagan, and Anna Mayo, Vita Giorgi, and the Narrator, the race of gossip, and *The Intimate Diary of Solitude* were all around.

Mariquita Samper's Childhood

She was born in San Juan, Puerto Rico, like her mother, Berta Singerman. Uriberto Eisensweig and Berta Singerman had a daughter named Mariquita Samper—according to the Narrator. Mariquita was the illegitimate child of Uriberto and Berta—he added by way of gossip. The fact that Mariquita was born on her mother's 50th birthday was also scandalous. And that, from day one, she was born independent of her parents. I don't like dependence—she said. Mariquita was born talking. And the whole world was shocked. Not only was she born talking. She was born rocking from north to south, and from east to west. Mariquita was a child prodigy. She sang, read, laughed, cried, spoke, ate, wet, pooped, burped, and napped. She was a child prodigy like her mother—said Berta. After her father raped her when she was 15, Mariquita fell in love with another guy, also called Uriberto. It was he who told her that she should write the script of *The Intimate Diary of Solitude*. The Narrator chose Mariquita as his protagonist at first sight. Although Berta had taught Mariquita to be foolish, Mariquita wasn't frivolous like her mother. Mariquita and Berta were very different. Berta was much more frivolous than her daughter—said Giannina. I, having lived in both of their bodies, affirm that there is no comparison. I would go so far as to say that Berta wanted to destroy her daughter. But it was Mariquita who destroyed Berta—said the Narrator.

And she destroyed her because she did nothing to destroy her. No, nothing except steal her lover—said Giannina. And what do you call that? Nothing? I would agree—said Mariquita—that I did absolutely nothing. Life took care of it all. You know—said the Narrator—that life takes many turns. And those turns bring many surprises—said Mariquita. Berta made me suffer, but I got my revenge. I stole her lover and then dropped him like a hot potato. I fell in love with another Uriberto. Forfeited my Russian citizenship and went to live in New York. Acquired American citizenship. And disgraced my mother and father. Then the Narrator suggested I write a book entitled *Mariquita Samper's Childhood.* He'd pay me a million dollars for the rights. I'd have to say that I had a miserable childhood. In short, I portrayed myself as an orphan. My parents are thugs—I said in *Mariquita Samper's Childhood.* Of course, I became a heroine to the American public. Little Orphan Mariquita. Daughter of those filthy thugs who stripped her of her American citizenship. And yet, in spite of all its lies, the book was a best-seller in the U.S. and Russia. Remember—said the Narrator—that Mariquita had asked for asylum at the Russian embassy. She wrote a letter to the Russians stating that she wanted to be a communist. She had been mistaken. She had realized the value of Russian citizenship, especially as a Puerto Rican. My confusion lies in the fact that I'm a sad colony. Don't you see that I'm Berta Singerman? Don't you see that I'm confused? Don't you see that I don't know who I am? The Russians immediately granted Mariquita political asylum. And this was the story of Mariquita's childhood in *The Intimate Diary of Solitude.*

The Raise

Chewing gum and blowing a really big bubble, I dreamed and dreamed until I suddenly popped the bubble with my fingers. Then I started chewing with more zest and zeal. That was Mariquita Samper talking. Giannina Braschi told me that she'd put me on TV. I told her I wanted to go on the air, blow a big bubble, and pop it. That's how the cast of *The Intimate Diary of Solitude* would be introduced. I jumped and jumped for joy when Giannina accepted this number in her video. Uriberto, Berta, Giannina, Vita, Honorata, Anna, and the Narrator were there as viewers of *The Gum of Life*. Missing were Montserrat Nissen and Brian Pecanis. They had just finished making love. They turned on the TV and were watching *The Adventures of Mariquita Samper*. Mariquita was gone in a flash, and Brian seized the moment to lay a kiss on Montserrat, who was madly in love with her darling. You are my darling—Montserrat told Bran. And she sighed deeply. In the middle of the kiss and the sigh, the phone rang. Damned phone—said Montse—doesn't give us a moment of privacy. Even though we're the lost lovers of *The Intimate Diary of Solitude*. Montserrat answered the phone. Hello? Hello? Yes, Montse. This is Mariquita. Did you see me on TV? I'm calling to let you know that we're giving the Narrator a party. He just got a raise so that he can make a more extensive cinematic production. He won all sorts of grants. They're crazy about his cinematic novel. Of course—said Montse as Brian kissed her again. And Mariquita laughed. Hey, Montse, what's the matter? You're not paying attention. I'll call you back when Brian is not touching you in *The Intimate Diary of Solitude.* How did you know that we were making love? It's a cinch to guess your luck, Montse—said Mariquita. I'll call you later. I'm busy too. I've only got five seconds before I go on the air. We'll chat then. Bye, Montse. Five seconds later, Mariquita was back on TV. Montse—Mariquita said suddenly. Since it's so hard to talk by phone, I'm letting you know that the party won't be at the Narrator's house this time, but at Vita Giorgi's. I'll see you at eight o'clock, Wednesday night. Please bring five bottles of wine. Anna, Berta, Giannina, Honorata, Uriberto and, of course, the Narrator will be there. The camera zoomed in on Mariquita's smile, especially her gold tooth. My luck has changed for the better since I gilded my tooth. The Narrator cut out the scenes of the gold tooth and the raise. He had these prophetic words inscribed in gold letters on a big poster: "Making money is turning solitude into a diary. In other words, it's shit." Look out, Montserrat, something is missing. What's missing is a king-size bed to celebrate the love of the lost lovers of *The Intimate Diary of Solitude.* Good idea, said Mariquita through the TV screen. A water bed. I'm going to pierce it so they'll drown when it bursts. You're wishing me dead?—asked Montse. No, Montse, you're not the one I want dead. It's the Narrator and Uriberto even more. I'm fed up with both of them. I want to be as free as my white dove. Do you want some popcorn? She flashed her gold tooth again and stretched her hand through the TV screen, and

Brian took the popcorn and fed Montserrat through another kiss with popcorn and solitude, Mariquita, solitude. Then the lights went out. And only God knows what took place on the water bed that Mariquita popped with the pin of love in *The Intimate Diary of Solitude.*

Manifesto on Poetic Eggs

Success—said the Narrator—is the first poetic egg. Success and money. I don't worship you or respect you in the slightest—said Mariquita Samper. Your eggs aren't poetic eggs. Your briefcase and plastic smile don't fool me. A pack of police dogs should rip you to shreds. I object—said Uriberto Eisensweig. I object—said the Narrator. You've just laid a poetic egg. This wasn't written in the official script. But it's written in my heart—said Mariquita. Do you think you fool me? If you want to cash in on a novel, look for one of those cheap novelists who go around selling my dreams and poetic fantasies for big bucks. I wasn't born to be your puppet. I'm not here to make you wealthy with lies. I was born to tell the truth. All this cock-and-bull that novelists like you have told—stupid Narrator—has nothing to do with what really happens at the margins of existence. What about the crazy old bag lady in Central Park who digs through garbage cans looking for food? No one mentions her. Who the hell cares about Montse and Brian? Who gives a damn about your *Intimate Diary of Solitude*? I'm happy to say, nobody gives a damn. But it worries me that Little Orphan Mariquita should be paid a million bucks for telling her asinine official story. It's about time I flushed all this shit you've made me write. I'm not egocentric, you know. It's easy to recognize egocentric writers like you, Narrator. The first thing they do is establish "how-to" doctrines. What they're really after is power. Power and money. And they have a very strange way of looking at me, Mariquita Samper. They minimize life and the world. They're not lyricists or bohemians. They're propagandists, pushing pamphlets and doctrines. What's the matter? You didn't expect a Macy's makeup artist to say these things? Subversive? I'll always be subversive because the subversive always speaks the truth. What chapter were we on, Narrator? Read it all back to me to fulfill your literary ambitions. How much is missing from the chapter on poetic eggs to satisfy idiots like you? How many pounds of makeup must I put on to fool life? And, for the record, I am free. I chose to be a Macy's makeup artist. I love to smear my face with lies because the more pounds of makeup, the more life weighs, and the more revolutionaries like me will write revolutions and manifestos on poetic eggs. I flash my gold tooth again. And lie down to sleep. But I'm immediately awakened by solitude. Dear Narrator, your diary has me locked up in this solitude that says nothing of the intimate reality of life. Have you seen how black people dance in New York City? Their dance is like the dance of love. All I need is love. Love. Love. On the other hand, I maintain the form of poetic discourses and novels, but I'm introducing a subversive element. This subversive element is my heart, which contains a little golden worm that never lets me sleep peacefully and always tells me, "Mariquita, always walk to the left. But don't go so far as to lose sight of my heart's dance." After trudging through the city streets and watching all the lies, I go home at the end of a day of deep solitude and write the *Manifesto on Poetic Eggs*. There go the drooling writers and pamphleteers. Of course they make money. Of course they eat well. They talk with their tongues hanging out, just like you, stupid Narrator. Boom! Boom! He's dead. He's dead. Mariquita has killed the Narrator. Revolution in *The Intimate Diary of Solitude*. He's dead. He's dead. But he's not dead. He has just told me that he doesn't like aggressive women like me. He has just told me that there's too much resentment in my words. And he has just told me that I also say, "Boom! Boom!" and don't kill anybody. After all, I'm not a feminist. I don't have to be a feminist to call myself Mariquita Samper. I'm sustained by my name and my person. I'm an egg and nothing more. When I go home at the end of the day, they tell me that I've insulted my mother's memory. When I was a child writing poems and pitching them into the basket, my mother would say, "Mariquita, don't throw away what you write. Have some respect for yourself." She was right even though she was wrong. My mother wrote piles of shit and thought all of it deserved the name Berta Singerman. Her self-esteem overstepped the boundaries of fantasy. Berta thought she was more important than what she wrote. Her queen-bee attitude said it all. She never dreamed Mariquita would make fun of her. It never occurred to her that Mariquita lacked self-respect because she had so much respect for the writing of mankind and life. I don't matter. I'm just a machine writing the world and life. What matters is the *Manifesto on Poetic Eggs*. And this manifesto is anonymous. It was written by rain, wind, blood, and pain. It was written by Mariquita's gold tooth. Her red freckles and red hair are more important than Mariquita Samper. You just don't matter, Narrator. To quote your poster, "Making money is turning solitude into a diary. In other words, it's shit." A golden bird in my heart dictated these prophetic words. I read them before you in this conference of absent writers of New York.

This is all bullshit. And I denounce it. I won't be taken for a fool. I've been playing Mariquita Samper for too long. I quit! I'm leaving *The Intimate Diary of Solitude* forever. When I smile my Mariquita-smile, they say—How pleasant she is! She is truly the Queen of Beauty, Charm, and Coquetry—but now that I'm writing the *Manifesto on Poetic Eggs*, Oh! Oh!—they say—Watch out! Beware! Her eggs must be destroyed! They're eggs—they say. They're eggs. They're not poems. Not novels. Not plays. Not masterpieces. We must yank out her gold tooth. We must dislodge her freckles and cut off her red hair. No! Shitty lecturers, you won't destroy me! Mariquita ran away with her poster and her *Manifesto on Poetic Eggs* after dictating a death sentence to all the lecturers, writers, and novelists who had written *The Intimate Diary of Solitude.*

2. Rosaries at Dawn

What matters most of memory
Is the precious gift of conjuring dreams.

—Machado, *Solitudes*

The Building of the Waves of the Sea

I was walking as usual in the wide and foreign land of New York City when I saw from afar Bengal lights that erased distance and landed me in a building. I saw the Arts Cinema of *The Intimate Diary of Solitude*. Then I entered a magic world. I wound a music box, and out came Uriberto and Berta, Mariquita, and the Narrator—all dancing. I closed my eyes slowly to feel the fire of death. A few seconds later, I felt *Death of Poetry* was already over. I immediately pressed the elevator button. And its gigantic doors opened. I saw a skyrocket blast off on television. Then I dropped to my knees and prayed. I almost felt new. I had dreamed of constructing a big building in which many languages would be spoken. And I dreamed of a kingdom of steel. I saw some little butterflies, and I saw a bee and a grasshopper in the middle of them. I pressed a button and wound a music box. For a writer like myself—said the Narrator—to wind a music box is to fill a gas tank. And to allow a skyrocket to blast off in the middle of a phrase that suddenly finds itself stuck in traffic and to see from afar that memories get confused and their feet become cotton and foam comes out of their mouths. A few seconds later, I repeated a sound I had heard in the streets of New York. My hand trembled as I quoted the sound of night. I nearly died. Died from solitude. Actually, nothing had changed. *The Intimate Diary of Solitude* was full of people. The walls were covered with graffiti. It was all a photocopy or a recording from a long time ago. But I found the waves of the sea as I entered *Rosaries at Dawn*. I should have repeated the movement of the waves of the sea until I reached the farthest horizon. I pulled up the covers and lay down to sleep. I didn't want to go ashore. I should have dived directly into the closest and the farthest. People make mistakes—I told myself. They don't think of the sea as a building. But I'll prove that the waves of the sea reproduce the movement of life. In the city of *The Raise* everything repeats the rising momentum of the waves of the sea. Everything is gold sand and water flooding the gaze. I'm writing the movement of storm and sea, not poetry. I had fallen asleep with my eyes open. I had dreamed a pure dream. And I had left that dream free. I had pressed another button without the slightest feeling of guilt, and I had seen what I never had imagined I would see. As I was lying on the tomb of my bed, I envisioned the inside of *The Building of the Waves of the Sea*. It wasn't hard to go through the revolving doors. I put on my galoshes and raincoat, and through the revolving doors, I slid into the labyrinth of *The Intimate Diary of Solitude*. The first thing I noticed were the mannequins of Mariquita and Uriberto, Berta, and Honorata Pagan in the display window. It felt strange knowing that my manuscript was behind the facade of this building. It was almost as if the building's architect could go through its revolving doors and slide through the kingdom of his dreams. There were stores on every floor. Selling nickels, clowns, buffoons, shepherds, doors, nights, days, and doormen. It had the facade of New York City. And it looked just like an empire. Selling the movement of the waves of the sea. The way I saw it after it went up—said the architect—it looked like the island of Manhattan submerged in the movement of the waves of the sea. Although I had always dreamed of building an empire, it was rather strange to finally stand before it. I chatted with Uriberto and Mariquita at Caffé degli Artisti. Then I left and took a long subway ride across the city of my dreams. I went into another building. I needed to enter *Book of Clowns and Buffoons.* Now it was perfect. At least now I knew why the magician had destroyed the circuses. And why the fortune-teller had predicted that one of the drunkards would finish *Profane Comedy* after he freed himself from all of death's dreams. I made many mistakes, or laid many eggs, as Mariquita would say. But you learn from your mistakes. Some of the shepherds in *Pastoral* needed finishing touches. I redid their faces—said Macy's makeup artist Mariquita Samper. Sometimes the floor even shook. I spent hours in perplexity and pain. I feared that I'd die before I had sculpted all the wrinkles on the face of my building. I've spent many years building the life and death of these characters and of this poetic universe. I never knew that after the construction of *Profane Comedy* would come the realization of *The Intimate Diary of Solitude*. But the death of the shepherds in *Pastoral* and *Song of Nothingness* gave birth to *The Intimate Diary of Solitude*. With a helmet on my head and a drill in hand, I was a contractor. I called my employees together and told them that I wanted to build *The Intimate Diary of Solitude*. I paid them monthly with gifts. All the work was the artistry of dreams. I gave them instructions. A concrete ideology was unnecessary. There are no ideas in the world—I told them. We are not Marxists, or capitalists, or feminists, or whatever else is in fashion. If anything, we are workers for the empire of the poet-artist. And if we can identify with anything, it is with revolution. For which we had to destroy and rebuild ourselves. Our revolution is not about self-complacency. It is about constant self-criticism. We detest all kinds of egocentrism. We detest power, success, and especially the opportunists of the world. We are honorable men. And we are honored by work and the finished product. We do not love gods. We detest the infinite and immortality. We create the empire of the world and the empire of death. Life is born from death. From the death of *Assault on Time* came the birth of *Profane Comedy*, and from the death of *Profane Comedy* came the birth of *The Intimate Diary of Solitude*. And what will be born will later die. The dying will reach the limits of the undying. This is the poet-artist's doctrine that made the construction of *The Intimate Diary of Solitude* possible. This doctrine has the movement of the waves of the sea. I was born on an island, so every character acting in any show in this building also depends on the movement of the waves of the sea. We imitate the nature of the sea. Our building is a mirror of the life of the sea. My eyes have been lost in the movement of the waves of the sea ever since I was a child. My art is a product of this solitary movement that produces both storms and days of great peace and tranquility. It's summer for me on the island of Puerto Rico even though it's winter for us on the island of Manhattan. I am an Odysseus. And I say, as Odysseus once said, that the greatest feeling is going home after a long journey through the city of dreams. My art is the art of exile. I've raised *The Building of the Waves of the Sea* so I wouldn't feel further removed. I'm proud of having been born in this building and of having built each one of its stores. I wish you were as happy as I am. I make happiness work. I am the producer of happiness. That's why I'm giving you all my stores. I've created the sea, as well as movies, love, happiness, grief, clowns, cards, *The Raise*, the city of dreams, Caffé degli Artisti, *Manifesto on Poetic Eggs*, poetry, prose, night, day, elevators, doormen, sadness, solitude, joy. Mention whatever you want. I'll give you more things yet. I'm not done building this building. I've created three symphonies and have six left. I'm still gazing at the facade of my building. Forgive my rejoicing. It's not egocentrism or pride. It's joy. I'm the architect of this world, and I'm still not done with it. I think that all art is representation. Come to my place. You'll see I live alone on the 7th floor, and from there I see all that the world represents. It's winter outside. And it's warm inside my building. I'm still sliding with my galoshes through the city of my dreams. I'm about to go through other revolving doors into the bank of *The Intimate Diary of Solitude.*

Mariquita Samper's Financial Statement

I confess my financial state—said Mariquita Samper. I confess all that could have been different and was different. I confess all the things that I believed to be different from what they really are. All of *Profane Comedy*'s poetic eggs have constituted the fortune of *The Intimate Diary of Solitude.* Would you believe—Mr. Banker—that in *Book of Clowns and Buffoons* I went bankrupt? I thought I'd lose my mind. I had to take a sabbatical after I wrote it. I took a year off. And then I went back to work. I took out a loan for $2 million to write it. I ask myself—Our Father who art in heaven—if the financial statement of other writers is like mine. I have been mistaken so many times. And I confess my mistakes. All my losses have turned into enormous gains. Did you know that I lost all my earthly possessions for love? Or that I've already finished writing *The Building of the Waves of the Sea*? Or that I've just laid some more eggs because I thought that the building would come earlier? But see how strange poetic architecture is. You erect a building with the site in mind. And then you find out you're wrong. What is never wrong is the poem's logic. The building had chosen its own site even though I had thought it would exist somewhere else. The poet of *Assault on Time* used to call it *the mandate of things*—and I think she was right. Things choose their space. Things rule the world. They are in charge, even though you'd like to think that you can order them around. Of course—Mr. Banker—egocentrics don't understand this logic. They impose their own logic on poetry. And that is the basis for the explosion or the schism between the worlds of writers like Mariquita Samper, who obey the mandate of things and who are enslaved by writing, versus the writers who impose themselves on things. Of course, added the Narrator through Mariquita Samper's mouth, when you read the Berta Singermans of the world, you feel that they're derided by the very things they're trying to ride. They're killed by irony. That's why they never reach the category of deathless. Do you know what happens to them, Mr. Banker? From wanting to be above things, they end up underneath them. The writer who doesn't write, but allows writing to write itself, leaving things as they are, and erasing himself from the map of existence, remains ironically within them. This theory comes from the poet-artist's theory of the perishable. Only what is fated to die is capable of living. Only what dies lives. Why do you think Christ was killed? They killed him to prove that he wasn't a god. But in killing him, they immortalized the perishable and transformed man into a god. Remember Vallejo's verses? "The day I was born, God was sick." He also said, "There are blows in life like the hatred of God." Note, Mr. Banker, that Vallejo deprives God of his immortality. He humanizes God. Imposes death upon him. Imposes the perishable. God is sick, as I am. God hates, as I do. And in doing so—believe me, Mr. Banker, in humanizing him, what he does is immortalize his humanness. I'm not interested in gods, Mr. Banker, I'm interested in human beings. And yet, the gods envy my death. Gods can't create as I do because they're immortal and incapable of dying in order to be reborn. That's why they can't create different things. They're condemned to live the dream of the imperishable. I've told you many times that I'm a golden worm. I declared I was an egg in *Poems of the World*. Now I affirm that I am that egg. I've died many times, Mr. Banker. I've been destroyed time and again by the mandate of things. And I'll be destroyed over and over again. If I keep creating or laying eggs as I've done up to now, I'll have no choice but to be ready to die in order to be ready to live again. Amen. Forgive me, Mr. Banker, for mistaking you for a priest, but aren't you supposed to have economic healing powers? And I—Mariquita Samper—am just about broke. I'm a nickel. I'm the body of *Empire of Dreams*. I'm money. And I confess my financial statement. It's in pretty bad shape, eh, Mr. Banker? You remind me of the stupid Narrator. Allow me to pay you with a check. I still have something in my account. I'll see you tomorrow, same place, same time. Rest in peace, sinner. Rest in peace, Mr. Banker. And let me leave you. In peace. In peace. In peace.

Requiem for Solitude

Have you noticed how the characters in this book have disappeared? It's as if only the sea were left remembering the dreams of all these characters. A while ago, when I was at one with the sea with all my thoughts in its waters, I saw how the end of *Empire of Dreams* was filmed. All the characters of *Assault on Time, Profane Comedy,* and *The Intimate Diary of Solitude* were standing in the water. Holding burning torches. Illuminating the night. I couldn't make out their features because their faces were besmeared with makeup. But they spoke. Or rather, they made noises that caused the movement of the waves of the sea during the spectacle of the night. I'll never forget how there was no light except for the torches. Torches that looked as if they were suspended in midair because I couldn't see anyone holding them. All the characters were sighing or groaning or screaming or crying. They looked like souls torn from their bodies. And it wasn't because their bodies were torn from their souls, but because their souls had been torn from their bodies. And, above all, they wept. They were like abandoned echoes. Like the echo of seashells. Let's keep in mind that their voices simulated a chorus of echoes. And the idea of a chorus is essential. Because I felt they were singing *Requiem for Solitude.* And I felt they were living all its movements. Solitude is not a voice, just an echo. When I say that it's just an echo I don't mean that it imitates, but that it projects the voices of solitude with an unwonted repercussion. These characters were dead. And yet they had come to life. They were suddenly feeling the fire of death over the movement of the waves of the sea. They were bringing death's movement to their own movement, slowly, while the ship of fools sailed on. I'd dreamed of bringing to this rhythm a final dance that would invade the maritime continent of this book. But I'm not even sure what my writing is capable of writing. I'm the hand that writes the writing of the world. Other fragments that I haven't even noticed have passed by me over the waves of the sea. I'd like you to listen a while longer to the writing of the reading of this book. I still haven't found in the waves of the sea the end of the movement of the last wave in the outlet of the manuscript of life.

The Movement of the Waves of the Sea

How strange—said Mariquita Samper. And she went to the kitchen and turned off the light. Then she turned off the light in the living room and the dining room. Leaving only her desk light on, she looked down, closed her eyes, concentrated on one spot, opened her eyes, and saw that her pen was writing on that spot of the page. You see, I've felt lost watching the movement of the waves of the sea. I've touched the heart of a star. At other times of my life, the rising sea only gave voice to waves that came by storm. I've always written about the waves of the sea. They always assumed different voices when speaking to me. Even when they sensed that the fury of calm had come after the storm. Peace is airy. In the wake of the waves, everything can sound the same or entirely different. I often considered writing the fragment I'm writing right now, but it never came out this way. I'm afraid to lose what I'm writing. Things are what they are when they have already stopped being what they are. It's so strange. I'm writing this whole *Empire of Dreams* on my water bed. Sleeping. And writing while kneeling. Praying. But to write dreams as I'm doing now is to let the poetry-writer run and flood me with dreams and memories. I've never believed in time or dreams. What do people mean when they talk of existence? What is the basis for saying that I exist? What is the basis for saying that everything continues when everything is dead? In what book or fragment of world history is it said that men exist because they die? Has anyone really gotten close enough to existence to be able to say that anyone who exists without a notion of death exists without a notion of life? A curious idea just occurred to me. I'll let things swim over the waves of the sea for now. You shouldn't force the movement of the waves of the sea. Be at the mercy of things. Do you mean to tell me that if a wave knocks me down and drags me away, I should let it? Yes, you should stay wherever it leaves you, so you'll discover distance. Then I'm only a puppet of destiny. Maybe all of *Profane Comedy*'s clowns and shepherds came about this way. To be at the mercy of the waves is to be at the height of existence. To allow things to exist. I said that it was all so strange. Now I don't feel like swimming over the waves of the sea or under the waves of the sea. Do you know what I'm doing now? I'm floating. To survive is to float. Wait a minute. I don't like this stuff about surviving. I don't want to be above life. I want to be even with each moment of my life. And what do you think? To be floating with life is to be even with life? I could never do this before. And I'm not sure that in the near or distant future I'll be able to do it again. I'm not even sure that I'll be able to write another word. In my life everything is fortuitous. Everything is gratuitous. I used to impose order on things as part of my discipline. Now I let the sea's lack of discipline impose its discipline on me. It's all so strange. As a child, I devoured books. The same passion I had for reading I now have for writing. Now my reading has become my writing. I write the same way that my eyes penetrate someone else's line. By writing, I'm reading what I write. By writing, I used to read my past, my present, and even my future in my writing. Even when I walked along the sand of the beach this summer, I felt that I was reading as I was contemplating the sea in the wandering of my eyes. It was as if the infinite were momentarily condensed. The infinite isn't divine—it's human—absolutely quotidian and real. Even as I was writing this fragment, I felt that my grounds had been invaded. My writing's point of reference had nothing to do with my reading's point of reference. But my life has always been full of sudden changes. And I've had to include those changes in my writing. In the morning, I run through part of my building. Take a subway to another world, to another building. And then head back to my building as I'm walking through the life of the other building. Running through the city of dreams. I almost always know when I can and cannot write. Some books are written in anguish or despair. This book is written when I'm feeling lost. But even that lost feeling is lost. It's misplaced or transformed. In order to write how the sea moves, I've had to cry and I've had to suffer. As I was walking around New York City alone today, I walked into *The Intimate Diary of Solitude*. I had a cup of coffee at Caffé degli Artisti. I watched some clowns and buffoons who were performing the poem of the fortune-teller and the poem of the magician. Then I got lost in the labyrinth of dreams. I no longer felt my name was Mariquita Samper, let alone Giannina Braschi. I felt like losing myself on the seashore. And I lost myself in all the waves of the books that I've written. I didn't know where I was. This happens to me often. I came across Uriberto Eisensweig, who asked me to go with him through all the stores of my building. So I went. He changed his costume and dressed up like a shepherd. He asked me how he looked. I said he didn't look right. After being Uriberto you can never be a shepherd again. And yet, there were many other men who dressed like shepherds, clowns, and buffoons, and their costumes suited them well. The difference was obvious. We were in other periods of our lives. I feel I can now represent the movement of the thoughts of my solitude. The dislocation that I feel when I'm writing is part of the intimacy. Intimacy, deep down, is solitude. A toy began dancing in my diary. I didn't notice its movement when I was writing these pages in the building. It's true that things are beautiful when they work. Art is function. Forgive me for having danced so much. I always excuse myself. But my excuse is a way of imposing my way of thinking. Or of letting things impose their mandate. My handwriting adapts itself to the architecture of each one of my books. Let them dance. Or let them show the power of their movement. Only then will you notice the flash of their explosion. Soon they'll stop singing. And they'll die. Like the waves of the sea. And they'll rise again. Don't let them lie still forever. I've just run out of gasoline. At the end I always have to stop at a station. And fill my tanks. All that begins is an ending. And I say as a sailor once said in a romance of the solitude and the sirens of the sea:

> I only sing my song
> to whomever follows me.

About the Author

Photo Copyright: Michael Somoroff

Giannina Braschi is one of Puerto Rico's most influential and versatile writers of poetry, fiction, and essays. She was a tennis champion, a singer, and fashion model during her teen years before discovering writing. She lived in Madrid, Paris, Rome, and London before settling in New York, where she taught at Colgate, Rutgers, and City University. With a PhD in Golden Age Spanish literature, she has written on Cervantes, Garcilaso, Lorca, Machado, Vallejo, and Bécquer. Author of *United States of Banana* and *Yo-Yo Boing!*, Braschi's cutting-edge work has been recognized by the National Endowment for the Arts, the NY Foundation for the Arts, *El Diario*, PEN American Center, the Ford Foundation, Danforth Scholarship, Instituto de Cultura Puertorriqueña, and the Reed Foundation. She writes in three languages—Spanish, Spanglish, and English—to express the enculturation process of Hispanic immigrants—and to explore the three political options of Puerto Rico—nation, colony, or state. Braschi dedicates her life's work to inspiring personal and political liberation.

About the Translator

Photo Copyright: John Stuart

Tess O'Dwyer's English rendition of the Latino literary classic *Empire of Dreams* by Giannina Braschi won the Columbia University Translation Center Award and inaugurated the Yale Library of World Literature in Translation. She has also translated Giannina Braschi's novel *Yo-Yo Boing!* for AmazonCrossing. With a master's degree in literature from Rutgers, she edited *Review: Art and Literature of the Americas* and translated the nineteenth-century social realist novel *Martin Rivas* by Chilean author Alberto Blest Gana for Oxford University Press. Tess O'Dwyer's short story about her late Korean mother, entitled "Ballerina of Chestnut Mountain," won first place in the National Short Story Competition of the Hackney Literary Awards. She is a board member of PEN American Center, Evergreen Review, and Harvard University's Cultural Agents Initiative. She runs her own arts management consultancy in New York City.

Made in the USA
Middletown, DE
26 October 2018